THE ROOKIE'S GUIDE TO ESPIONAGE

AN EVA DESTRUCTION ESPRESSO SHOT

DAVE SINCLAIR

THE ROOKIE'S GUIDE TO ESPIONAGE

AN EVA DESTRUCTION ESPRESSO SHOT

A rookie spy. Europe on a knife edge. A distinct lack of coffee.

Eva Destruction is back in her first ever assignment. Straight out of the MI6 academy, Eva is on the trail of a supposedly dead fellow agent. It's a nothing assignment given to a rookie, but when suicide bombers hit a NATO conference the mission is kicked into high gear.

Eva chases a carnage of gunfire and explosions across Europe in search of the mysterious shadowy organization, 'The Tempest'. *The Rookie's Guide to Espionage* is a high-octane thrill ride that will keep you guessing until the very last page.

What others have said about Eva Destruction:

"As if Stephanie Plum had James Bond's (Australian) love child...I loved it. It's fun, it's funny, it's clever. I want a movie of this now. Brilliant."

CHAPTER ONE

Eva thought she'd been sent on a wild goose chase.

Then the bombs exploded.

She had been sitting outside a quaint little café in the Old Town part of Lyon, on the phone to Nancy, watching tourists leisurely traverse the winding cobbled streets. Her best friend was having trouble understanding why Eva was in France.

"Nance, I'm at a conference. It was a last-minute thing. Sorry I missed drop-the-pen-down-Patrick's-butt-crack Tuesday at the pub, but a spot opened up and I took it."

"Since when do baristas have conferences?" Nancy asked in her sweet Irish lilt. "What are you going to learn? The latest bean technology? What's new in mugs? How to grow pretentious facial hair?"

There was no way Eva could tell her best friend she was in Lyon because she'd accidentally joined MI6. Eva was now only a part-time barista. The remainder of her time was spent saving the world. Well, okay, just that one time. So far. The rest appeared to involve a lot of paperwork, and learning how to kill people with pencils. Her instructors were very focused on pencils for some reason.

Eva was in France in preparation for the NATO summit. Although her mission was slightly less sexy than that. There were reports a former MI6 operative had been spotted in the square where Eva now sat. This had piqued the interest of MI6 for several reasons. One, the operative hadn't left the employ of MI6 on the best of terms. Two, his appearance seemed oddly timed, given the impending summit. And lastly, he was meant to be dead.

Someone matching his description had been spotted by a member of the CIA and the report had been passed on to MI6. There were so many spies in the city, Eva wondered if there were any actual residents left. Although apparently there weren't enough MI6 operatives to spare for something this trivial, hence why they had assigned Eva.

Her mission was to search for the former operative and then, when her superiors were satisfied there had been no further sightings, head back to SIS Headquarters at Vauxhall Cross in London.

Eva was sure she'd been assigned because it was a bullshit lead, but an assignment was an assignment. A once-dead operative in the vicinity of a NATO meeting was quite a coincidence. MI6 didn't like coincidences. Or swearing. Or tattoos. Or back talking. It was amazing Eva had a job at all.

"You know I love my husband more than pizza," Nancy said, "but my god, sometimes I think he could be outsmarted by a large capricciosa."

Eva laughed. Nancy always made her laugh.

"What's he done now?" Eva asked. "Is this about the amazingly good deal from that dodgy Latvian guy? Did he end up getting the side of lamb?"

"Oh, he got it alright. And it was a side. Plus another side, and the front and the arse," Nancy said, sounding equally annoyed and amused.

"So… what did he buy?"

"A lamb. A whole one. A whole live one."

"*What?*"

"Right now, he's in our lounge room eating a cushion. We're calling him Steve."

Eva laughed again. It was the perfect cover. To passers-by she appeared like any other tourist talking on the phone to a friend. Because that's exactly what she was.

The sun glistened off the golden statue of the Blessed Virgin Mary atop the Basilica of Notre-Dame de Fourvière. It was a perfect day.

Until the explosions.

The first explosion blew apart the marketplace. The deafening roar came a split second after the flash, then debris, smoke and flames spewed into the sky. Fifty metres from where Eva was situated, hell itself was unleashed.

Eva realised she still had the phone to her ear.

"Are you still there? What's going on?" Nancy was yelling. "That sounded like an explosion."

Eva's focus snapped to what had to be done next. "Coffee machine malfunction. I'll call you back." She hung up without waiting for Nancy's reply.

Disorientated, Eva tried to process the event. Her first instinct was to run toward danger, a characteristic that often got her in trouble. People scrambled in all directions. Many ran from the growing plume of dread. Others, braver ones, ran towards it, to help those who had been innocently buying fresh produce mere seconds before. Chaos reigned.

The screams were the worst. Fear mixed with agony, and cries for loved ones no longer able to answer their anguished pleas. The only sirens were those of car alarms. The other sort would come soon enough.

Eva was on her feet; the shock had worn off. She was in fight mode, ready to sprint into the fray. Her training kicked in, and she took her first tentative step towards the carnage.

The second explosion blew her off her feet. Far closer than the first, the shockwave sent Eva tumbling. The third came seconds later. The explosions wiped out those who had rushed towards the madness, cutting them down in a blinding detonation. Market stalls and humans alike were torn apart, engulfed in fireballs of terrible force. The screams intensified.

Eva had witnessed the cause of the final blast. Amid the carnage, a young man who couldn't have been older than sixteen calmly pressed a button attached to a backpack. An instant later, he'd been vaporised.

The three suicide bombs had decimated the peaceful tourist precinct of Old Town Lyon. All that was left was devastation, the dead and the dying.

Eva had to help the wounded. She got to her feet and broke into a run, weaving through the throng of terrified people scrambling away from the chaos. One woman clasping an expensive handbag to her chest slammed into Eva, dislodging the phone from her hand. It clattered on the cobblestones, shattering the screen.

Eva pushed on, leaving her phone behind. People needed her immediate care. Headquarters could wait.

Amid the terrified mass, one person caught Eva's attention. More precisely, one person's hand. A young man, roughly the same age as the youth who had detonated the last bomb, ran towards Eva, his thumb frantically pressing a red button attached by wires to his backpack.

A fourth bomber.

Eva drew her pistol and skidded to a halt. Planting her back foot, she fired three times into the air. Even in the frenzied rush, the crowd froze. Except one person. The bomber sprinted away from Eva, snaking through the now-stationary crowd.

Eva aimed at his head. Given he had an explosive device strapped to his back, it seemed the safer option. Her gun traced his movements, waiting for a clean shot.

Ahead, she spotted was a gap in the crowd. Eva would have her chance. But as the bomber reached the edge of the gap, a bearded man carrying his daughter stepped into the line of fire. Eva lowered her gun, unable to take the shot.

Ball nuggets.

Eva broke into a run, determined to not lose her prey. She followed him into the narrow side street.

Her first priority was to make sure he didn't sacrifice any more innocent lives. Plus, he could provide vital information if taken alive. Eva thought back to why she'd been in the square in the first place. Her mission had changed. Eva was now on the tail of a terrorist. And she was gaining on him.

Lyon was one of the worst cities in the world for a street pursuit. The city was a labyrinth. One Eva didn't know. Old Town had over 300 secret passageways, most behind unlocked doors. Despite this, the bomber's course was amateurishly straight. No double backs, no detours to mask his intent. It was like he'd been shot out of a cannon.

So much for a cruisy first assignment. Having been at MI6 for a year, Eva had only recently graduated to field work. She was still learning the ropes. Turned out there was more to spycraft than knowing how to mix a martini.

The kid was either unfit or the backpack was heavier than it appeared. Probably both. *Good.*

A straight section of paved street stretched out before them. Eva had her chance. She stopped and lined him up in her sights, then took the shot, followed by two more in quick succession. All three missed their mark. Her prey didn't break stride, and tore around the corner. She recommenced her pursuit.

Cursing herself, Eva sped up. She was normally an excellent shot—just shy of Olympic qualifying, apparently. This was due in part to her MI6 training, but mostly to her emotionally abusive douchebag ex-boyfriend, who used to own a firing range. Running and shooting with any semblance of accuracy was next to impossible. A steady hand and controlled breathing were key. Eva had no such luxuries.

The pursuit surely hadn't gone undetected. The explosions had rocked Lyon. A plume of ugly black smoke hung over the city like a portentous spectre. A young man wearing a backpack with wires hanging off it, being chased by a woman with a gun would surely have been called in. Eva had to make sure she reached the bomber first. The last thing she needed was a trigger-happy gendarme shooting a terrorist and accidentally exploding another bomb —and her.

Eva ran on.

She passed cafés and high-end boutiques. She flew past couples wearing scarves and berets. If she spotted someone carrying groceries with a baguette hanging out of the bag she'd have to yell at them for being a cliché. Eva shook her head. She had to focus.

She darted through the narrow cobblestoned streets, her hours at the gym paying off nicely. Her quarry was a mere 30 metres ahead now, and she was gaining on him with every stride. The young man threw a panicked glance over his shoulder.

Eva may have been a freshly minted spy, but she was accustomed to danger. Explosions and gunfire were all too familiar—in fact, she'd been shot at far less since becoming a spy. That was a concerning thought; one she'd have to digest another time.

Rounding a corner, the bomber skidded and diverted his course. Something had spooked him. As she turned the corner, Eva saw why. Two police cars had pulled up and blocked his path. Gendarmes were clambering out, fumbling for their guns.

The bomber scrambled sideways, watching Eva approach. The three young frightened gendarmes traced his erratic movements with their guns. Their eyes were wide, fear etched on their features.

"Arrêt!", one of the young police officers yelled, his voice cracking.

The bomber didn't hesitate. He sprinted toward a side street and away from the Eva. The gendarmes traced his movements and aimed.

They were going to shoot him in the back. More specifically, in the backpack. The one that contained a very explodey bomb. Not only would they lose their only living bomber, they'd take out everyone in the area, including themselves.

The cops hadn't noticed Eva's advance. With only a split second to act, Eva made a rash decision. Her forte.

With a panicked eye on the terrorist, one of the cops yelled, "Tirer!" and the rest tensed.

Still sprinting, Eva levelled her gun. Her target bounced in her vision, making precision virtually impossible, but she did her best to control her aim. Three shots in quick succession roughly hit their target. The front right tyre of the police car exploded, collapsing the front of the vehicle. All three cops turned their guns on her.

At least she had their attention.

The bomber careened toward the corner. Eva followed. She flung her gun arm backwards and fired into the windscreen of the cop car. The three gendarmes dove for cover.

Over her shoulder, Eva yelled, "Pardon!" and waved an apologetic hand.

She silently prayed the police would be slow to react. Eva didn't want to wind up shot in the back instead. Not only would they be shooting the wrong person, but they'd mess up her smooth, unblemished skin. Eva was quite fond of her bikini bod; bullet holes would definitely cramp her style. Then again, so would death.

Thankfully, no shots rang out. As she skidded around the corner, she saw that the bomber was still within striking distance, though the gap had widened. As if suddenly noticing the labyrinthine streets, the terrorist diverted from his straight path and tried a nearby door. It could have led to a hidden passageway, or it could just as easily have been someone's garage. He lucked out and dove in.

The bomber must have assumed he'd lose his pursuer in the warrens of the city, and she'd simply give up.

He didn't know Eva.

She tore the door open, raised her gun and scanned the low passageway for threats. It was empty. Ten metres down, it split into three. Two of the paths shone with sunlight, the other was dark as a crypt. Eva slowed her pace and controlled her breathing, focused on sound; any sound.

At first there was nothing but the slight sound of the city. Traffic, the faint sounds of sirens. Then, the slightest shuffle, the movement of a shoe, or a backpack against a wall.

Got you, you little cockwomble.

The darkest passageway. Of course. She edged her way down, listening intently, her pace careful, gun at the ready.

Eva pulled back the hammer of her pistol, but it was all for show. She was a good agent, she'd counted her shots. She was out of bullets.

No ammunition, no phone, no backup. If only she had a pencil.

Her eyes finally adjusted to the semi-darkness. There he was, wedged against the wall like a spider. Just like a spider, being cornered didn't make him any less deadly. Eva wasn't about to take her eyes off him.

Her weapon raised, she edged forward, mind racing. Her options were limited. The bomber relaxed his shoulders ever so slightly, perhaps suspecting what her hesitation meant.

His face descended into a scowl. "You should go home while you can. Stay there for a long time. A war is here. You are not prepared to withstand the oncoming tempest."

Eva stopped her advance. "That's where you're wrong." Her smile made him take a step back. "I am the oncoming tempest."

"Mere words. What could possibly make you the tempest?"

"We haven't been properly introduced. The name is Destruction. First name Eva."

The bomber grunted. "Eva Destruction? You sound like one of those Bond girls."

"Been one of those, don't recommend it."

Amusement drained from his face. "What do you think is going to happen now, little girl?"

"Little girl?" Eva's hackles were up.

"You with the gun, pretending to be like a man."

"You're right, this espionage stuff is really hard. My vagina keeps getting in the way."

A derisive snort. "So you are one of these forceful women, then? One that demands everything?"

"No. I'm a woman. Welcome to the 21st century. We have smartphones, gay marriage and, like, eleventy billion ramen restaurants. Enjoy your stay."

"You have a very smart mouth."

"It's kind of my thing. Now, back on topic, what do I think is going to happen? I'd like to say you put down the backpack and we go have a hot chocolate, but I'm guessing that's not on the agenda."

"It is not."

"Not a hot chocolate fan?"

The bomber grasped the red button, but still nothing happened. Unintentionally, Eva let out a snicker. That only made him press the button more frantically.

She don't know what three-year-old had constructed the bomb, but their soldering was as useless as the g in lasagne. She eyed the dangling wires, thankful for their ineptitude.

The bomber followed her gaze. His head snapped around, trying to inspect the backpack, like a dog chasing its tail. He managed to grasp two of the dangling wires, a menacing sneer smeared across his mouth.

Stupid, stupid, stupid.

As the youth twisted the wires together, Eva backed up. A beep from the bowels of the backpack didn't bode well. The bomber grinned at Eva as he fumbled for the red button.

Eva turned and ran.

She managed to open the ancient door and leap outside before the explosion engulfed her and she was propelled forward. The world turned dirty orange and black, and the edges of Eva's vision became ashen. Flaming debris, screams and smoke wrapped around one another in a terrifying cacophony of the senses.

Eva had one last thought before she blacked out. She hadn't called Nancy back.

Everything went dark.

CHAPTER TWO

Eva awoke with a scream.

She fought to move her arms and legs. As Eva's eyes adjusted to the light, she saw that she was tied to a wooden chair in the centre of a stark room. The only illumination was from a solitary bulb in the corner of what appeared to be a basement. This was no police cell.

Eva smiled. *Classic.*

It was such a textbook example of Interrogation 101, it was almost cute. If this was meant to intimidate her, they had thoroughly failed. This set-up might work on a petty criminal, but Eva was quite familiar with interrogations, and was made of far sterner stuff.

The plastic ties were irritating, though. Handcuffs were easy to escape from. Lock-picking was one of her hobbies—she always carried a bobby pin, just in case. Once upon a time, before becoming a 'respectable' spy, Eva had led a less-than-illustrious life. Picking locks had been part of her regular routine. But the plastic ties were problematic. She had far more experience with handcuffs—and not exclusively in a professional sense.

A slight cough caught her attention. Eva twisted her head to get a view of her captor. The lone woman was tall and slender, jet black hair cascading down her long, elegant neck. She held herself with confidence.

"I am glad you are awake," she said with a painted-on fake grin. "It is not much fun asking questions of someone who is unconscious, no?"

The woman's French accent was thick, but she took care to enunciate every syllable. Eva spoke fluent French, but would stick with English for now. You could learn much from someone who may struggle to choose the most appropriate word.

The woman moved forward so Eva wouldn't have to strain to see her. "I apologise for your current predicament. I'm afraid my employers insisted."

Eva tilted her head. "And who might your employers be?"

The tiniest crease of amusement appeared for an instant in the corners of the woman's mouth before disappearing just as quickly. "Let us just say they are interested in your involvement in the incident in the square..."

Eva noted she didn't use the words *terrorist incident*.

"... but regardless, I do not agree with you being manacled."

With a shrug, Eva said, "If I had a dollar for every time I'd been strapped to a chair..."

Her captor raised an eyebrow, as if waiting for her to complete the sentence.

Eva thought. "I'd have, like, twelve dollars."

The woman frowned. "This does not seem like a lot of money."

"Do you think I should consider raising my prices?"

"You 'ave a sense of 'umour." The woman folded her arms. "You will need that in the 'ours to come."

It wasn't a threat, more a statement of fact. Eva envisaged torture in her near future—unless she did something about it. She sized up her captor.

"You've done military service, but that was some time ago. Am I right?"

The woman tilted her head, but offered no verbal response.

"It's the way you stand, rigid, like you're at attention. Your accent, your flattened consonants, means you're from—"

"I 'ave 'eard this about you," the woman interrupted. "You like to analyse people, hmm? This is a good gift to 'ave, to read people, I think."

"You… you know who I am?"

"Yes. You are Eva Destruction. My organisation 'as a file on you. Keeping an eye on spies is nothing new, of course. But we 'ave been monitoring you for quite some time, for different reasons, of course. Your entries before you joined MI6 were, shall we say, more colourful, yes?"

This was a turn-up. Not only did they know she was a spy, they knew about her life before she'd become one. Her criminal exploits back in Australia were hardly worthy of international interest. That meant they had been tracking her ex.

Was that why she was here? Enough of being on the back foot. Eva needed answers.

"So where are you from?" Eva asked. "I'm going to take a wild stab and say DGSE?"

The DGSE, or General Directorate for External Security, was the French equivalent of MI6. The more likely candidate to talk to Eva was the DGSI, the French domestic equivalent to MI5 or the FBI, given that the event had taken place on home soil. But that wasn't Eva's assumption.

"Pardon?" The woman appeared genuinely surprised.

Eva had her. "The fact that this isn't a formal interrogation and there's no one around to record it means this is either an officially unofficial DGSE interrogation or my library fines are way more out of control than I thought."

The woman frowned approvingly. "I see now why MI6 'ired you." She traced her finger slowly along Eva's jawline. "You are more than just a very pretty face. My name is Isabella Beart." She ran her thumb over Eva's bottom lip. "And I do indeed work for DGSE."

Eva did her best to ignore the intimate caresses. "Then you

know I'm your ally, your friend. And friends don't usually tie each other up."

Isabella tilted her head and pouted. "Depends what type of friends you 'ave, is it not?"

"Look... that's a really good point, and one I'd usually be making, but..."

The DGSE agent folded her arms. "Ms Eva Destruction, you were seen cavorting with a known terrorist, Mustafa Khoury, formerly of Lebanon, recent resident of the 'ousing estate Rose des Vents in Aulnay-Sous-Bois."

"*Chasing* a known terrorist. Slightly different to cavorting."

"We 'ave witnesses stating you were protecting the terrorist. You fired on gendarmes."

"Sure, if you want to talk facts."

"Friends do not shoot at friends usually, hmm?" As if to reinforce the point, she pulled a PAMAS pistol from her jacket. The message was clear. While admiring the pistol, she said casually, "So, my question to you is, why is MI6 assisting terrorists?"

Isabella was an experienced interrogator. One second she was flirting, the next she pulled a gun. Keeping the subject off kilter would normally be an effective technique, but not on Eva. She knew all the tricks, and she was losing patience.

Eva sighed. Her options were limited. The DGSE weren't her enemy, so there was no point fighting her way out. She had nothing to hide. She gave Isabella a concise rundown of events. She retold the incident with the gendarmes repeatedly, until Isabella finally seemed satisfied that Eva had been protecting the police rather than aiding a terrorist. She made sure to include the part about the oncoming tempest.

That caught Isabella's attention. "So this was not isolated? There is more to come?"

Eva nodded. "I got that impression. At least, that's what he believed."

"Huh." With that, Isabella left the room.

And left Eva strapped to a chair, unable to move, without food or drink and, more importantly, without a toilet break.

Forty bladder-crunching minutes later, Isabella returned. She didn't appear happy.

"I 'ave spoken to my superiors," she said emotionlessly. "You are to be executed for treason the day after tomorrow."

"What?"

Isabella frowned. She pulled a small, slender device from her pocket and pressed a button on the side. The flick knife sprung to attention. Isabella held the knife to Eva's neck and ran the flat of the blade along her soft skin. "This is joke. You like jokes, do you not?" She brought her face close to Eva's, inhaling her scent slowly. Isabella traced the blade along the length of Eva's leg, then in one quick movement, cut away her leg bindings.

With Eva's hands still bound, Isabella sat astride her. "My superiors believe we should be partners. They 'ave contacted MI6 to request this."

Wriggling her arse into Eva's lap, Isabella ran the knife along Eva's cheek, slowly, lovingly. "You shall make an excellent partner, I think," she said, her hand caressing Eva's neck. "Yes, an excellent partner indeed."

One moment Isabella was staring into Eva's eyes, the next she'd leapt up and cut her wrist ties. Eva wasn't sure if the semi-seduction was part of the act or the true Isabella. Time would tell.

Eva hoisted herself up unsteadily and rubbed her wrists, then stretched and cracked her back. Being stationary for so long never agreed with her.

Isabella stood back and admired her. "I am curious. What will the amazing Eva Destruction do next, I wonder?"

"Pee," Eva replied matter-of-factly. "Then get coffee. Then catch the bad guys." She pondered for a moment. "Yeah, definitely in that order."

The lavish surrounds of the Cour des Loges was a welcome change of scene. The warm, candlelit restaurant was far removed from the dingy basement where Eva had been interrogated. Having enjoyed a glorious five-course degustation, she wiped her mouth with a stiff white napkin and conceded defeat. The five-star hotel was a milieu Marie Antoinette would have felt right at home in. Despite being so full, Eva still wanted to order the cake.

The juxtaposition between interrogation and indulgence was as stark as it was swift. One moment Eva had been strapped to a chair, the next she was in a luxurious hotel suite taking a soothing bubble bath while drinking expensive champagne. She was surprised she didn't have whiplash.

Isabella leaned back in her chair, seeming to approve of her companion's gratification. She refilled Eva's glass without asking. "This Frascati is amazing. I buy it by the crate from Italy. It is extremely un-French of me, no?"

Eva shrugged, unsure how to reply. Isabella pulled out a silver cigarette case and lit one with a match.

Eva was aghast. "Can you do that here?"

Isabella regarded her curiously and surveyed the empty restaurant. "I think you will find there are different rules for the DGSE."

"But you haven't been able to smoke in a French restaurant for at least a decade."

Isabella frowned in acknowledgement and took another drag. "So this is not your first time in France?"

Eva assumed Isabella knew that wasn't the case, but decided to play along. For now.

"No, not at all. I have a place here."

"A place?"

Eva shrugged. "Well, more like a castle. In the Rhone Valley."

Isabella laughed, then saw Eva's face. "You are serious?" It seemed she wasn't as well-informed as she made out. "You 'ave a castle? Why on earth would you work at MI6 if you 'ave such a thing?"

"It was a gift. I didn't earn it. If you know anything about me then you'll know I make my own way. I'm not one to sit back and just take things."

Her companion took a long, slow draw of her cigarette and let the smoke dance over her tongue. "But sitting back and taking things can also have its benefits." She hefted a suggestive eyebrow. "It can be most pleasurable, no?"

Her flirting was incessant. The fact that it had continued long after the interrogation told Eva it was no act.

Eva toyed with the remains of her crème brûlée and tried for a casual tone. "You know I'm straight, right?"

Isabella poked out her tongue and used her finger to delicately remove a speck of tobacco. She fluttered her eyelids seductively. "So is spaghetti until it is 'ot and wet, hmmm?"

Eva rolled her eyes. "I've seen that meme too."

"I 'ave found that memes, like lies, work best when they 'ave an element of truth."

"And spies know all about lies."

"That is our business, no?"

Here was Eva's opportunity to bring the conversation back on track. "Speaking of business, what do you know about the attacks so far?"

A small *huff* of disappointment told Eva that Isabella was reluctant to be brought back to work. *Too bad.* Lives were at risk, and Eva had nearly died. She wanted answers. She wanted revenge.

"My people are examining CCTV footage from nearby businesses and train stations, as well as footage from personal recording devices. We 'ave profiles for three of the perpetrators and are working on background motivations."

"You've IDed them already? Any known links to terrorist organisations?" Eva asked.

Isabella paused to ash her cigarette. "Not that we can find, but it is early days, yes?"

Eva frowned, impressed. "I wouldn't say that. You've identified them already. Your people work fast."

"My people are 'ighly motivated. The incidents today cost over one hundred lives. My country is sick of such acts of violence. We will stop at nothing until we know who did this. That is what we do."

Eva rubbed her wrists. She had no doubt about the lengths

Isabella and her people would go to. "Pretty sure it'll top the agenda at the NATO summit."

"This is a sensible assumption."

"May I use your phone? I need to check in with MI6."

"But of course." Isabella retrieved a phone from her handbag and handed it to Eva. "They 'ave been informed of their operative's good 'ealth."

Eva nodded. She didn't ask if they had also been informed that said operative had been strapped to a chair and grilled like a criminal. She highly suspected they hadn't.

Eva excused herself and found a quiet little alcove in the majestic surrounds of the old hotel. After multiple transfers through untraceable connections she was finally put through to her handler.

"Thank Christ, Evie. I've been worried sick."

Just hearing his voice made Eva feel safer. Paul Cavendish had been her handler, mentor and voice of reason since her first day at MI6. He was also one of her closest friends.

He also happened to be Nancy's husband.

That Nancy didn't know either of them worked for MI6 was something they weren't comfortable with, but they were actively complicit in the deception. They were spies, after all. Eva was sure the truth would come out one day; she just hoped she wasn't nearby when it did. Or that she at least had access to copious amounts of alcohol.

She gave Paul a fast rundown of her experiences, and very scant details about her interrogation, which she referred to as 'slightly aggressive questioning' on the DGSE's part. She'd delve into that particular protocol breach another time. Firstly, because there were more important things going on, and secondly, because she was speaking on Isabella's phone. She didn't know who was listening in.

Paul listened intently, asking only the occasional question. When she finished, Paul gave her a rundown of MI6's understanding of the events. This matched the DGSE's in almost all aspects. Except for one.

"We've had a breakthrough they haven't," Paul said with a detectable note of triumph. "The last bomber, your good friend Mustafa Khoury, is either a world-class idiot or we've been amazingly lucky—possibly both. We ran the photos of the perpetrators through our database and hit a match. Mustafa passed through Heathrow six months ago, under the alias of Akram Nazari. From there, we just traced the use of that identity and matched it with the known facial features and Bob, as they say, is your uncle." There was a crunch, as if Paul was eating a biscuit. "Vienna."

"I'm sorry?" Eva asked.

"Vienna, that's where your mate Mustafa was two days ago—at a pretty fancy hotel, I might add. A simple credit-card trace. Like I said, world-class idiot. He used the same identity to book the hotel, and paid with the same card—three weeks in advance, by the way. The Viennese authorities jumped on it, and the hotel's CCTV footage confirms it. It's the same man."

"Boy," Eva corrected him.

Paul ignored the comment. "In light of your new partnership I thought you'd like to be the one to drop this piece of intelligence. It will be good to suck up to the cool kids at the new school with a sweet new pogs."

"Dude, how old are you?" Eva asked, laughing.

"Old enough to know about pogs, apparently, and how you're missing out if you're not part of the cool crew."

"Wow. I'm seeing a whole new side of you."

"You're welcome."

"I didn't say it was a good thing." Eva was thankful for his efforts to cheer her up.

Paul's tone turned grave. "Evie, you need to be careful." There was a pause, as if he was selecting his words carefully. "I want you to be wary of your new friends."

She let her silence ask the next question for her. Far across the restaurant, Isabella extinguished the last of her cigarette and perused the dessert menu. She seemed oblivious to the conversation, but Eva couldn't rely on that assumption. That sort of thing got you killed.

18

Thankfully, Paul continued without prompting. "It's almost like someone knew what was going to happen. The DGSE had the profiles all lined up and ready to be released. Any faster and they'd have been circulated beforehand. It could be down to good police work..."

The unfinished sentence said much.

"But you don't think so?" Eva asked, really hoping Isabella's phone wasn't bugged.

There was a long pause. "No, I don't. This thing smells fishier than Billingsgate Fish Market."

Eva was intrigued that Paul had reached the same conclusion she had, albeit for different reasons. She was a rookie, but an experienced agent like Paul sharing her doubts made her feel validated. Isabella should be eyed with caution. The interrogation and the incessant flirting, combined with Paul's well-honed scepticism, put Eva on edge. She would have asked more questions, but it wasn't a secure line.

If Isabella, and possibly the DGSE, weren't to be trusted, the next logical question was why? The DGSE was renowned for its professionalism and integrity. What reason would one of the top spy agencies in the world have to lie? It didn't add up.

Eva decided they were questions for another time. "Am I to assume I'm no longer looking for a dead MI6 spy?"

"If you pass him on the street, give me a call, otherwise this is your primary, secondary and tertiary mission. Two cabinet ministers were among the dead. The Prime Minister is out for blood, and the king has issued a strongly worded statement. He even used the word 'miffed', so you know he's pissed. The stock market has tanked and the Euro is worth less than my last bonus. The entire world is searching for answers, Evie, and right now you're the prime candidate to bring home results. No pressure, but I've put my lily-white arse on the line to keep a neophyte on the case. We need results, and we need them fast."

Paul must have swung some hefty influence to keep her rookie arse in the game. It was a lot of pressure, but the one thing that made an impact was that her friend had her back. That was all she needed for motivation.

"Seeing as I've been Shanghaied into this cross-agency arrangement, can I ask that you book me onto the next—"

"Flight to Vienna? Already booked. Accommodation, transport, surveillance and weapons packs will all be awaiting you on arrival. I'll text the details to Ms Beart's phone as soon as we're done. I'll require daily updates. You're booked under the name of Chlamydia Phlegm."

Eva sighed. "No I'm not."

"No, you're not." Paul chuckled. "But that would be a pretty good code name, don't you think? I'll keep that one on file."

She had to smile at her friend's continued attempts to cheer her up, even though it had only partially worked.

"Keep your tuchus out of harm's way, Evie. I don't want any awkward conversations with unnamed parties."

He wasn't referring to the MI6 hierarchy; Paul was talking about his wife. He rang off and Eva returned to Isabella, who was enjoying another cigarette.

"How was Cavendish? I 'ave 'eard 'e can be quite priggish."

Eva did her best not to smile. She'd seen her friend singing *I will Survive* while standing on a bar, dressed as a unicorn. Priggish he wasn't.

"He's a good egg. Not priggish. He's actually quite modern in his opinions, especially about advancing women in the Secret Service."

With a blank face, Isabella extinguished her cigarette. "There are two universal truths about the modern male. They are nowhere near the feminist they think they are, and their toilet aim is far worse than they think."

Isabella made a good point. Not wanting to discuss Paul further, Eva changed the subject. She gave her new partner the news about the alias, credit card and Vienna link.

Isabella's reaction was one of genuine surprise. Either that, or she was a world-class actress. Eva hoped for the former. After a few phone calls that was that, they were off to Vienna. The French spy picked up her handbag and headed for the front entrance.

Eva glanced at the table. "Don't you need to pay the bill?"

Isabella scoffed, then inspected Eva's face. "Oh, you are serious?" She shook her head. "We have different rules in the DGSE."

Eva nodded, rubbing her wrists again.

Isabella continued. "As we are to be partners, there is one thing you must know about me." She ran her fingernail down Eva's bare arm, giving her goosebumps. "Rules, they are for the unimaginative, the wearisome and the classe inférieure. They are boring!" She elongated the last word. "We will 'ave much fun, you and I. Fate has drawn us together, but misery acquaints a man with strange bedfellows, yes?"

Eva knew the quote. *The Tempest.* "You know Shakespeare?"

"Personally? Non." Isabella wrinkled her nose. "But I am aware of his work. Just as I am aware you are no man, Eva Destruction." She slid her hand across the small of Eva's back. "Come, we 'ave only just started our journey. You and I will be great partners."

Eva wasn't sure if that would turn out to be true, but one thing was certain. Her time with the DGSE agent would be anything but boring.

CHAPTER THREE

The Hotel Imperial wasn't your regular terrorist hangout—not that Eva had been to many terrorist hangouts. The majestic Viennese hotel wasn't your regular tourist trap, either. The hotel's opulent surrounds, complete with marble statues and extravagant crystal chandeliers, were enough to make even a Kardashian step back and say, 'Woah, tone it down, dude.'

The flight to Vienna had been uneventful, if Eva ignored the less-than-subtle innuendo from her travel companion. During take-off Isabella advised that her "landing strip is all clear". She mentioned the benefits of "'ead in the clouds", and upon landing she whispered that she "loved going down". At times Eva wasn't sure if her companion was a spy or a fourteen-year-old boy.

Eva still was uncertain if Isabella was flirting because that's who she was, or if the DGSE agent was trying to keep her off-balance.

Regardless, Eva had a mission. The English press was in a frenzy about the cabinet ministers. Terrorist incidents were news-worthy enough, but with well-known politicians involved, the press were baying for blood. And a rabid English press was not a pretty thing.

As they sat in the palatial surrounds of the hotel foyer, Isabella impatiently tapped her foot. They had been waiting for the hotel manager for an hour. Meanwhile, hotel life went on about them, with elegantly dressed staff flitting about the aging clientele like remoras tending to elderly sharks.

Across the marble floor came the *click-clack* of sensible shoes. A prim woman marched towards them. She was dressed in a crisp pantsuit, her black hair tied back in a severe bun, her make-up thick, but perfectly applied. She looked like a stern governess crossed with Posh Spice.

After curt introductions, the manager said in accentless English, "I understand you wish to gain access to one of our executive suites?"

"That is correct," Isabella stated in a manner that clearly conveyed her feelings about being kept waiting for so long.

"I'm afraid that is quite impossible at the current time." The manager's face remained unmoved.

Between clenched teeth, Isabella asked, "And may I ask why?"

"Are you an Austrian citizen?"

Eva stepped in before Isabella lost it. "I'm Australian, that's close enough, right?" Her joke received no response. It was as if the woman was made of Botox. Eva could see where this was going. She added, "No, we're not."

"No. You are not." The manager placed her hands behind her back and rocked on her heels. "You have no jurisdiction here. You may not have access, but I am able to ensure that suite 513 remains unbooked, at great expense to the hotel."

The manager's tone suggested she expected them to bow in gratitude. There was no bowing. There was also no expense. Paul had advised Eva that the bomber had booked the suite for three weeks. Either the manager was ill-informed, or she was deliberately misleading them. Looking at the prissy manager, Eva suspected it was the latter.

The manager continued. "Until such time as the legitimate authorities present themselves, I will not let any Tom, Dick or Harriette into our suites without a warrant. Hotel policy."

The good old "just following orders" defence. Their combined credentials meant nothing to her. Why would they? Spies were nothing new to Vienna.

A neutral country, straddling the divide between the East and the West and close to the Balkans, Vienna had always attracted secretive types. Austria had the most liberal spy laws in the world. Spying itself was not illegal unless it directly targeted Austrian interests. The place was basically a stock exchange for information.

Vienna was a city of secrets.

Surely there had to be a human somewhere underneath that thick veneer of make-up. Eva decided to try a new direction.

"Look, we're obviously all working women here—"

"Working, yes, but you two," the manager eyed their outfits, curling her upper lip in disdain, "appear to be from a whole other profession."

She didn't mean espionage.

Eva chose not to respond to the slight. "Listen, I know rules are import to folks like you—"

"Like me?" the manager spat. "What do you know about me?"

Eva assessed her, from her sensible shoes to her tight bun. "I know you reek of self-loathing, like someone who acts in infomercials for a living."

Both the manager and Isabella stared at her in disbelief. Isabella was the first to move, placing a hand over her mouth to stifle a giggle.

Posh Spice had riled Eva. They weren't getting into that room today. The manager had been wasting their time.

She wasn't done. "I don't know why you're so unhappy in life. Is it because you realised Donkey Kong isn't an actual donkey?"

The manager vibrated with anger, and her face grew steadily redder. She was about to blow her tightly wound bun.

Isabella plastered on her best fake cordial sneer. "Thank you for your time," she said, and ushered Eva away.

Eva was aghast. She hadn't even used her good material yet.

The manager swivelled and marched back to her office. Despite her anger, Isabella's gaze followed the woman's arse as it snaked towards the door. *Definitely gay.*

"Come on," Isabella said as she shoved her partner along. "We should 'ead back to our 'otel. We will not get in the 'otel room today. Let us go."

"I'm not letting the likes of that," Eva pointed a thumb in the direction of the manager's office, "determine if we succeed or fail."

"Then what...?"

With a wrinkle of her nose, Eva said, "Give me a minute."

Eva calmed herself and guided Isabella towards the luxurious couches facing the hotel bar. As they sat down, Eva selected an option on her new phone and waited for the software to download. The phone had been issued in her weapons pack on arrival.

She hadn't really needed the hotel manager's permission, although it would have been easier. Now they had to be sneaky. They had to be spies.

They sat in awkward silence, like an uncomfortable married couple.

"If you could travel to anywhere in the world right now," Isabella began, "where would it be?"

Eva was intrigued by the change in topic. Clearly they were past the 'And what do you do?' stage. Eva had been to so many amazing destinations. She'd seen more of the world than most. And not the tourist-checklist spots, either. She'd been to many out-of-the-way exotic locations. But none of those were her answer.

"There's a place a couple of hours away from my home town, called Jan Juc."

Isabella nodded approvingly. "This sounds very French, I think, yes?"

"Not really. It's a surf beach. I go there and the world falls away. It's my safe place. You have one of those?"

Isabella nodded. "I understand the world falling away part. A little café, overlooking a park near my parents' 'ome in Créteil. I used to go there when I was a child. I was bullied in school and it was my safe 'aven. It always made me feel protected, like a womb, yes? Ever since, I go there to make sense of the world, to feel safe.

It is very special to me. We have these places 'alf a world away from one another, but I think we are similar, you and I."

"Maybe we are, Isabella," Eva agreed.

Eva thought this was a good opening to get to know her companion. On the brief flight to Vienna all their conversation had been about the mission—well, that and Isabella's frequent innuendo. Now they had a few moments of downtime, it was time to figure out who she was really working with.

"So," Eva began. "When I was nineteen, I was in love."

Isabella crinkled her forehead, as if wondering where the statement had come from. "Was it a girl? Is this your way of coming on to me? I must say it is about time. It 'as been a whole twenty-four 'ours. I was believing I 'ad lost my touch."

Eva grinned. "His name was Chad."

"Boo."

Eva chuckled and went on. "He was my world. I was beyond smitten. I'd given everything up for him. University, my family, my friends. Pretty much every dollar I earned was put towards our future. But when you're in love none of that matters, right?"

Isabella said nothing, but nodded for her to continue.

"Here I am, madly in love with the bloke who I'm going to spend the rest of my life with, and he suggests we get a little kinky."

Isabella leaned forward. "Please use as much detail as possible."

"He suggests we tie each other up. I, of course, agreed. I'm always down for that sort of thing."

"I am taking mental notes."

Eva ignored her. "Chad is all loving, strips down and handcuffs me to the bed. And then..." Eva sighed. "Then he went and made a sandwich."

"What? I think this is quite a foolish man."

"I know, right? When he came back, he was fully dressed. He pulled out our suitcases and started loading them up with everything we owned." Eva shuddered at the memory. "So, picture me, chained to the bed..."

"I can think of nothing else right now."

"… and screaming blue murder while he casually packs up all *our* worldly possessions. Takes the lot. All my books, my CDs, my clothes. Everything. He cleaned out my purse, took my cards and cleaned out my accounts. He… was not a nice person." A slow exhale. "I'd like to say that was an isolated incident, but I don't like to lie."

The truth was, Eva was gun-shy of any new relationship. Not just the likes of Chad, who littered the battlefield of her dating life like the first day of the Somme. The main reason was her recent ex had scarred her like no other man had, and hoped, ever would again. It would take an amazing person to make Eva trust once more. She would, but only when she was ready, and more importantly, when she could be certain the person wouldn't manipulate her into being someone she wasn't.

Eva caught herself. Did she just say person? She meant man, surely? She did, didn't she? She was pretty certain she did. Yeah, of course she did.

It was refreshing for Eva to be free of relationship dramas. A rare occurrence. She knew it would be temporary and she'd soon be back on the battlefield once more. But for now, she was thankful for the reprieve, or lull in the eye of the storm, or whatever it currently has was.

Isabella frowned. "I am unsure what it is you are saying."

"What I'm saying is I have some trust issues. That, and I make *the* worst choices in men."

"Maybe that is your meaning?" Isabella ran her fingers down Eva's arm. "That men are the problem."

"No, that's not my point at all. It's that people have to earn my trust, over and above normal folk, simply because of my past. I don't know you, Isabella, I don't know you at all. I know you're a flirt, that you're good at what you do, but I know nothing about you. Tell me something that defined you."

Isabella gave a slight shake of her head. "You are a very strange spy, Eva Destruction."

Eva shrugged. She wasn't going to argue the point. Folding her arms, she waited for Isabella's response.

"'er name was Alexis," she started, staring off into the middle-distance. "She was everything. A spy, like me, but also unlike me in every way. She was smarter, braver, more loving than I could ever be. I was temperamental, 'ot 'eaded, hmmm? I made rash decisions. She calmed me, made me focused. She made me a better person, no?"

"This story doesn't sound like it's going to have a happy ending. Go on."

"We were on a mission together. Our superiors, they did not know of our love. We were after a state scientist who was selling a small amount of nuclear material on the black market. We underestimated him. I was meant to have Alexis's back, but I rushed in like an impetuous child. I was not covering my partner when things went bad..." There was a long pause. "She died."

Eva saw the earnestness on Isabella's face. She was on the verge of tears. Her gaze remained resolutely on the other side of the room. Was this the true Isabella?

Eva placed her hand on the spy's knee. "Why did you tell me that story?"

Isabella sniffed, then straightened her spine as if hardening herself. "You see? I too 'ave learned from my mistakes. I would never let my partner down. My new partner should know this."

Not quite knowing how to respond, Eva nodded. "I have to get back to work."

Isabella pouted. The old Isabella seemed to have returned. She ran a finger along Eva's thigh. "Such dedication. I wonder if you pursue all things with such passion?"

Eva gently moved the French woman's hand away and held up a finger to silence her protest. With the same finger, she told her to wait.

She would digest Isabella's story later. She was relieved to know there was a more human side to her partner. It would make working together easier. But she put it aside for now. Eva had a mission.

Eva rose and walked towards the bar. On the way, she tapped on her phone.

There was no way Eva could leave the hotel without answers. There were so many questions. How did Mustafa afford such a place? And why Vienna? The city had centuries of spy history, but why would that appeal to terrorists? Perhaps it made it a logical meeting point for them. Eva didn't think so. There was something else at play here.

It was all supposition and gut feel. Eva had to provide more than that. There was a lot of pressure from her superiors at MI6 who thought hiring an Australian was ludicrous even before they met the mouthy, tattooed feminist. They had little faith in her abilities.

Then there were Isabella and the DGSE, who were probably of the same opinion. Eva could feel Isabella's gaze boring into the back of her head and knew she had to succeed in order to gain the trust of her new partner.

Eva was never one to be defined by the opinions of others. She had a mission. She had a clear objective. She would prove to the grey haired, blue-tie set that she was a great secret service operative. That she deserved her position and their respect. Eva would show them all.

Spurred on with a righteous fire in her belly, Eva cleared the last of the stairs up to the bar with a spring in her step. Unfortunately, there was a bit too much spring, and she tripped over her own feet. With her phone in her hand she stumbled and went sprawling into a table of four middle-aged businessmen. Empty coffee mugs, plates and laptops went flying. Eva bounced off the table and landed ingloriously on her arse.

Elegant AF.

Issuing multiple apologies in each of the three languages she knew, Eva backed away from the stunned businessmen. Not watching where she was going, she tumbled into an elderly couple sharing a rather large cocktail at another table. The sprawling table dance and profuse apologies played out all over again.

The entire bar must have thought she was drunk. The shock on

Isabella's face mirrored the appalled expression on those of the guests. Worried hotel staff rushed over, pretending to be concerned for Eva's welfare, anxious to stop the crazy lady from bumping into their patrons.

Eva raised her arms, claiming to be fine, but as she did so, she bumped into a third lot of people on her way out of the bar. The scathing glares burned her back as she stumbled away. Isabella stared at her in stunned silence. Eva ignored the gaze, flicked her hair and motioned for Isabella to follow her out of the bar.

When they reached the far end of the foyer Isabella appraised her partner with grave concern. "Are you... Are you alright?"

Eva ignored the question. "We're going to search the room."

Isabella gave a slight shake of her head, clearly confused. "Did you not 'ear the manager? We are not authorised."

Eva tilted her head. "You don't strike me as the kind of person to seek permission, Isabella. Didn't you say rules are for the unimaginative? You're not all talk, are you? Is it possible I've misjudged you?"

"Now who is teasing?" Isabella smirked. "But 'ow would we do this? We have no key."

Eva winked at her companion and called a number in her phone. It was answered almost instantly. "Hey Trev, got a job for you. Check my phone, I've scanned several... yep that's the one. Hotel RFID keys... Can you... yep. Room, 513... Thanks. Text me when you're done. You're a champ, cheers."

She rang off, enjoying the confusion on Isabella's face. Eva couldn't help smiling. Isabella must have thought she was clumsy and unprofessional, colliding with hotel guests. In fact, she was the complete opposite.

Eva had researched the hotel on the taxi ride over. The online reviews raved about the convenience of the RFID room keys, which gave guests the option of using their cell phone as a key.

Eva explained to Isabella that she'd turned her phone into a RFID scanner. Each time she'd bumped into a guest, she'd skimmed their room key information. She'd have at least five codes. Trev, the IT boffin at MI6, was currently pulling apart the data so he could provide Eva with a range of codes to find the one able to break into Mustafa's room.

Isabella's admiration was clear on her face. "Impressive."

"You should see what I can do with a pencil."

"I would very much like to see what you could do with a pencil. I feel I would find it, stimulating, no?"

"Don't flirt with me, I'm working here."

"Oh, I'm not flirting." Isabella raised an eyebrow. "If I flirt with you, you will know it."

Eva's phone vibrated in her pocket. Trevor had already cracked the codes. He had a range of frequencies; all Eva had to do was hold the phone up to the door and she'd be in.

They got in a lift and Eva hit the button for the fifth floor. As they ascended, her mind wandered. Why had the terrorist been in Vienna? He was a French citizen, why would he need to come to Austria? And why an expensive five-star hotel? Why would he want to stand out? Where did he get the money to pay for three weeks in advance?

The name "suicide bomber" tended to indicate he wasn't planning a sleep in and an à la carte breakfast. So why book the room for so long?

So many questions. It was time Eva found some answers.

The elevator pinged and the doors opened. The cream wooden panelling and gilded edging of the fifth floor screamed opulence. At a thousand Euros a night, you'd hope so.

Another thought pushed its way into Eva's mind. Why did Isabella seem less eager to search the room? Didn't she think they would find anything? If so, why come all the way to Vienna? Why give up so easily when faced with a prissy hotel manager? Eva decided that was a question for another time.

Room 513 had a "Do Not Disturb" sign on the door. Eva held her phone to the touchpad and waited for it to cycle through various frequencies. She was disappointed she couldn't show off her lock-picking skills, but technology moved fast, and she had to move with it.

A tiny beep on her phone was followed by a click of the door. Success.

The door opened silently and the two spies drew their guns. The suite was large. Ridiculously so—you could fly a few zeppelins around and still have room left over. Several doors led off the main room, indicating multiple bedrooms. Large glass doors opened to a balcony at the far end.

With her gun ready, Isabella nodded to the nearest door and motioned for Eva to follow. They cautiously entered the room, covering one another, scanning for any threat. There were none.

The smell of stale food permeated the room. Discarded chocolate bar wrappers and empty condom packets littered the floor. Someone had been having a good time.

Isabella placed her gun on the bedside table and began opening drawers. They were stuffed haphazardly with clothes. Why would a suicide bomber leave clothes behind? It didn't add up.

Eva was about to mention this to Isabella when she heard a *click* behind her. It wasn't any old *click*. It was quite specific. It was the metallic *click* of a pistol. They weren't alone.

Eva turned to see a person of short stature in the doorway. He couldn't have been more than five foot. He wore a stylish grey suit and vest, and his facial hair was trimmed and neat. Eva would have considered him rather dapper if he hadn't been holding a gun on them.

Two guns against one would have been far better odds, but with Isabella's gun out of reach on the bedside table, their chances were less favourable. Plus, the man had his gun trained on Eva and hers at the floor. He had a considerable advantage. Talk was the better option.

"Hi there," Eva said cheerily. "You're just in time!"

The man raised a curious eyebrow, but said nothing.

"Yes," Eva continued, realising she had no idea where this was going. "Uh, just in time to help us, ah…"

Eva glanced to Isabella for aid, but the DGSE agent just gazed at her, confused. She had no idea what Eva was on about. That made three of them. The man ignored Eva's floundering and stepped forward.

"Good afternoon, ladies, my name is Herr Ludger Volmer," he said in heavily accented English. "I work for the Bundesamt für Verfassungsschutz und Terrorismusbekämpfung."

Eva shook her head. "I'm sorry, I'm going to have to ask you to repeat that."

"I wish you wouldn't." The slightest hint of delight crossed his lips. "You may call it BVT for short. It is the Federal Office for the Protection of the Constitution and Counterterrorism, similar to your FBI or MI5."

"Well, that's lucky, we're from—"

"I am aware of your employers," Volmer said, cutting Eva off. "But I do not think you are authorised to enter this suite, Fräulein Destruction and Fräulein Beart?"

"I assume the hotel manager told you we were coming?" Eva tucked the gun into the back of her jeans.

The man shrugged, then nodded, acknowledging Eva's gesture, and lowered his own weapon. "That's a nice girl. You ought to go careful in Vienna. Everybody ought to go careful in a city like this."

With a heft of an eyebrow, Eva said, "Did you just quote *The Third Man*? That's impressive."

The man's face lit up with a genuine grin. "You know that movie? This is excellent. I use that line often and no one understands that it is from the film. You are my new best friend. Now, as my new best friend, tell me, are you Isabella or Eva?"

"Eva."

"Ah, exceptional. I am most pleased to meet you." He extended his hand and they shook. "I assumed the manager would not be able to dissuade you from coming here."

He nodded to Isabella, but did not offer her his hand.

Volmer continued. "I gave her explicit instructions not to allow any other law enforcement up here, local police included. One cannot set a trap if too many people are trampling it, yes?"

"Trap?" Eva asked. "For what?"

As if on cue, the front door clicked. The short man moved like lightning. Through rapid hand gestures, he motioned for the other two to hide, their weapons at the ready. It was doubtful it would be hotel staff. Another agency was possible, but so was another member of Mustafa's team. There had to be a reason the room had been booked so far in advance. That reason may have just walked in.

Though the newcomer couldn't be seen, the footsteps seemed cautious, tentative. This was not the stride of someone who worked at the hotel or had booked the room with nothing to hide. The footsteps went past the room they were in, down the hall to another.

Volmer motioned for them to follow and put a finger to his lips. He peeked through the crack in the door. Nodding to indicate the coast was clear, he tiptoed around the door, pistol raised. Isabella and Eva followed, adopting a similar stance.

Edging forward, the three entered the hall. Eva controlled her breathing, finger on the trigger. She remembered her training. She also remembered her mistake back in Lyon. There was no room for slip-ups now. Whoever had entered the suite could be their only lead. They couldn't lose this suspect.

Creeping forward as silently as possible, the three stalked towards the sound of movement. Without warning, a young man emerged from one of the bedrooms, his back to them. He was of a similar age and complexion to Mustafa. Under one arm he carried a pile of clothes. The sleeve of his bright red shirt was pulled over his other hand, and he wiped the hotel desk with it as he headed towards the kitchen. In his mouth was a half-eaten muesli bar.

Given the circumstances, Eva thought her cough was extremely polite. The young man spun on the spot, panic smeared across his features. When he saw the three guns trained on him, he jumped backwards and dropped the bundle from his arm. The muesli bar stayed put.

His hands shot up in the air and his eyes darted to a small machine pistol Eva could see laying on the bed. Like Isabella minutes before, he'd been caught off-guard and unarmed. *Diddums.*

As he took in the scene before him, his mouth gaped and the muesli bar tumbled from it. Eva could understand his reaction. With two sexy spies and a person of short stature, they must look like the cast of a 70s TV show.

It was Volmer who spoke first. "We apologise for startling you, Herr…"

The newcomer seemed disinclined to supply his name. His gaze flitted between the three of them and the front door, the only means of escape. His options were limited. A cornered man was a desperate man, and desperate men made stupid decisions. Eva kept her gun trained on his chest, her finger never straying from the trigger.

The kid stood stiff, tense, then moved backwards to rest against the couch, trying to look casual. He attempted an air of tranquillity, but it was a façade. He must have accepted there was no way out. He pointed at the muesli bar and raised his eyebrows, as if asking if he could pick it up. Volmer gave a slight nod.

The kid returned the nod and slowly reached down for it, keeping his eyes on the three of them. His shoulders relaxed slightly.

He took a bite of the bar. "So what is this," he said, waving the muesli bar at them. "You look like an improv comedy troupe of some description."

Eva preferred the 70s TV show analogy. His English was heavily accented with a French inflection. He knew what a comedy troupe was. The casual manner was forced, the sharpness in his eyes betrayed him. The guy was panicked but smart. His eyes kept darting to Isabella, probably because she was the main obstacle between him and the door.

Eva said, "Perhaps you could tell us your name?"

The young man smirked. "Justin Bieber."

"Look, dude," Eva used what she hoped was a soothing tone, "if you don't want me to shoot you, you're off to a terrible start."

The kid gave a slight chuckle, but said nothing further.

"Okay, Justin," Eva said. "Maybe you could tell us why you're in this suite?"

"I am robbing it."

"I see," Eva said calmly. "So you came all the way from France to break into a hotel room in Vienna. Sounds like a pretty inefficient thief if you ask me."

"My methods are not your concern."

"No," Eva conceded, "but your welfare is. As you've probably figured out by now, you're outnumbered and outgunned. And this one here," Eva nodded to Isabella, "has an itchy trigger finger."

"Yes, they call me Itchy," Isabella said, her voice dripping with contempt.

Eva eyed Isabella. "No, you don't want people to call you Itchy."

"Why not?" The DGSE agent appeared confused.

Eva gave a slight shake of her head. "You just don't. Trust me."

"What's his name?" Justin nodded to Volmer. "Mini Me?"

"Being shot in the kneecaps is just as painful as being shot anywhere else, sir." Volmer aimed his pistol at Justin's crotch. "But for you, I can always aim slightly higher."

Eva was losing control of the situation. "I think everyone needs to calm the fuck down, okay?"

In a slow, deliberate movement, Eva took her gun and tucked it into the back of her jeans, then raised her empty palms. The kid was too valuable to have this many weapons trained on him. She gestured for the others to do the same. Reluctantly, her comrades followed her lead.

Justin's shoulders relaxed, but his eyes remained vigilant, searching for any escape. He had to know there wasn't any. Cornered by representatives from three separate governments, his options were limited.

"So," Eva said nonchalantly, "how do you know Mustafa Khoury?"

The sudden jolt of his head said far more than any verbal answer could. He knew Mustafa, and was shocked Eva knew his name.

THE ROOKIE'S GUIDE TO ESPIONAGE

"I... I don't know anyone by that name," Justin said, his voice cracking.

Under his breath, Volmer said, "I think our friend here needs to attend some of those improv classes. He lies like a cheap Chinese watch."

"You've been caught clearing out the rooms of suspected terrorists." Eva planted her fists on her hips. "I think you'll find working with us will mean—"

Justin scoffed, interrupting her. "A war is coming to this place. Nothing you do here will halt the oncoming tempest."

There was that word again. *Tempest.*

Eva was about to ask more when there was a noise from behind her: the distinct *click* of the suite door being opened. All three spies pulled their guns and aimed them at the new threat.

The door opened slowly. The prissy hotel manager gawped at them in shock. She flung her hands in the air and the tray she'd been balancing went flying. As it clattered to the floor, Eva turned to see Justin flip backwards over the couch.

He rolled across the floor then broke into a sprint, headed directly for the balcony. In seconds Isabella had her gun trained on him and fired two shots. The balcony door shattered. The hotel manager screamed.

Eva shoved Isabella's gun upward. "Don't shoot him!"

They needed him alive. A bullet in the back would make getting answers slightly problematic.

Without breaking stride, Justin leapt through the shattered glass door and out onto the balcony, his three pursuers close behind.

Volmer raised his gun as he ran. "Where does he think he's going? He is five floors up, it's not like he will..."

He stopped mid-sentence as Justin leapt over the balcony railing. The jump was perfectly aimed and he landed on another balcony, diagonally across and one floor down. He rolled away, out of sight and out of range.

"Merde!" Isabella spat.

Her angry glare drilled into Eva, who ignored her rage.

Arguing about not shooting Justin, their only live lead, could wait. Catching him couldn't.

Eva was fit and limber, but parkour was not her bag. Neither was breaking her neck. But she wasn't willing to let their only lead disappear.

She took several steps back and leaned into a crouch, sucking in deep breaths as if she were about to dive into the sea. Except there was no water to break her fall.

Volmer was wide-eyed. "Are you mad?"

Eva winked and leapt into the void.

CHAPTER FOUR

She landed on the balcony with a sickening thud.

At least she landed. More accurately, at least she landed before hitting the unforgiving concrete below. There'd been a good chance of missing the small balcony altogether, but she'd made it, with no small amount of luck.

In a move that would make a paratrooper proud, Eva controlled her roll and was on her feet in seconds. She would have congratulated herself, but then she saw Justin's face. He was in the hotel suite, having jimmied open the balcony door. His stunned expression was all the congratulations she needed. Clearly he hadn't thought anyone would be insane enough to follow him.

He didn't know Eva Destruction.

Recovering quickly, Justin stumbled through the hotel room, heading for the door. As he went, he flicked furniture behind him, creating an obstacle course.

"Fräulein Eva!"

Eva glanced up to see Volmer standing on the edge of the balcony above. He threw a cell phone and she caught it.

"Isabella is on her way down to the ground floor. I cannot keep up. I will call you on that. Go!"

She didn't need to be told twice. Eva ran, hurdling the ornate chairs and lamps strewn across her path. The heavy hotel door hadn't fully closed by the time she reached it. She wrenched it open and bounded into the hallway just in time to see Justin slip into the stairwell at the end of the hall.

The screech of an alarm assaulted her ears. She saw why. On his way to the stairwell Justin must have punched the fire alarm. The glass had been smashed, and the red metal lever was down. *Clever boy.* Confused and panicked people milling in the lobby would only aid his disappearance. But he had to get there first.

Within a few bounds, Eva was in the stairwell. Even over the alarm she could hear Justin's frantic footsteps descending. Taking four steps at a time, Eva reached behind her back, but her gun was gone. It must have dislodged during the landing. When she returned to London she'd need to fill in all sorts of paperwork, but for now she'd just have to take Justin out the old-fashioned way.

And yet again, she didn't have a pencil.

Increasing her pace, Eva hoped Isabella would be able to make it to the ground floor before her. She would hate to tell her superiors she'd let the lone witness slip through her fingers a second time. She had two more floors before that could happen. Eva quickened her pace.

You're mine, you little badger fluffer.

It wasn't to be. As Eva passed the sign for the first floor, light flooded the stairwell below. Justin had reached the ground floor. After a final sprint, she burst into the lobby. As suspected, confused guests meandered towards the exits, unsure if the alarm was real. Eva couldn't see Justin or Isabella.

"Eva!" Near the front entrance, Isabella jumped to be seen over a group of Asian businessmen. "Over here!"

Before Eva reached Isabella she saw a faint glimpse of red. *Justin!* He was walking as fast as he could without drawing attention to himself, heading towards the kitchens. Away from Isabella.

Eva changed her trajectory, careening around an elderly couple, and motioned for Isabella to follow. Together they sprinted towards the kitchen. Thankfully the crowd had thinned in that area, and the closer they came, the fewer obstacles they encountered.

They surged through the swinging door. Isabella had her gun ready. Eva was armed only with her wit and her devastating fashion sense—a heady combination. Sweeping for threats, they found none.

The kitchen was abandoned and eerily silent. Pots of food, still steaming, stood on the stove. Vegetables lay half diced on counters. The staff had left in a hurry. As they made their way carefully through the kitchen, Eva picked up a large carving knife. Sure, her wit was cutting, but this was slightly sharper.

A rudimentary search determined that Justin wasn't in the kitchen. They exited via a rear door into startling daylight.

A group of white-hatted chefs sat on milk crates smoking cigarettes. They didn't seem too fazed by the alarm. Eva approached them, and in stilted German asked if they'd seen a man in a red shirt run past.

A rotund chief responded in perfect English. "He went that way," he said, pointing towards the main thoroughfare. "He seemed to be in an awful hurry." He appraised Isabella. "Now why would such a man run away from a woman such as this?"

"The world is a mysterious place," Eva replied.

"May I have that back?" the chef asked, nodding at the knife in Eva's hand.

"Sure," she said, handing it back, then she took off. She'd done so much running in the last twenty-four hours. These foot pursuits were playing havoc with her heart rate, but they'd be doing wonders for her butt.

With Isabella on her heels, she sprinted onto Vienna's main thoroughfare, the Stubenring, where wide, tree-lined streets circled the old city. Trams and cars motored along at an unhurried pace, unlike Eva and Isabella.

"There!" Isabella called out, pointing.

There was Justin, head high, sprinting along the footpath. Shocked pedestrians jumped out of his way. Luckily, he was easy to spot in the crowd. The bright red shirt had definitely been a bad choice.

The two spies sprinted down the street, dodging pedestrians and dog walkers. The DGSE agent seemed fit, keeping pace easily and hardly straining for air.

She gave Eva a sideways glance. "I could have taken him out," Isabella spat.

"And that's why I stopped you. We need him alive."

"Of course alive! What do you take me for?"

Eva didn't have an answer to that. Glimpses of red among the crowd kept them on target. They ran on.

The phone in Eva's hand rang. Without missing a step, she answered. It was Volmer.

"Where are you?" he asked.

As she crossed an intersection, weaving through slow-moving traffic, Eva glanced up at the nearby street signs. They told her she was at the intersection of Schubertring and Himmelpfortgasse.

With a grunt, Eva replied, "A street."

Volmer found the answer less than helpful, so Eva did her best to pronounce the tongue-twisting Austrian names.

"Ah!" Volmer proclaimed. "He appears to be headed toward the Danube."

"He's on foot, but moving fast, with a significant head start," Eva panted, still running. "I need to do something to improve the odds."

She hung up and veered off the sidewalk. Eva zipped between cars braking for a red light and made for the tramline centre strip. Isabella followed, her forehead wrinkled in confusion.

Passengers were alighting a tram at a nearby stop. Now was Eva's chance. She leapt aboard and headed towards the front. Isabella was with her every step of the way.

"This is your solution? A tram? James Bond, 'e never use a tram."

"He also never had hair like this." Eva flicked her head for effect. Her hair was totally on-point today.

Isabella frowned, reluctantly conceding the point.

The tram jolted as it took off, causing Eva to momentarily lose her footing. Isabella steadied her so she wouldn't fall. When Eva reached the driver's cabin she knocked on the perspex window. The young woman at the controls kept her eyes forward and scowled, as if she didn't like interruptions.

Eva knocked again and said, "Entschuldigen Sie," impressed at her retention of high-school German.

The driver continued to ignore her, but the scowl intensified.

"Allow me," Isabella said.

The metal clang against the window caught the driver's attention. The gun retained it.

"Relax," Eva said. "We're not here to hurt you."

"Is this a hijacking?" the driver asked in perfect English.

Isabella snorted. "Of a tram?"

"It could happen." The driver seemed hopeful.

"We are law enforcement officers in pursuit of a suspected international terrorist," Eva said, getting back on topic. "Over there, in the red shirt. We need you to miss the next few stops to keep up with him."

The driver sat up in her seat, apparently revelling in the excitement. They were gaining on Justin. Thankfully, he was keeping to the main thoroughfare, seemingly with a final destination in mind.

Eva heard a *tap tap tap* and turned to look at Isabella. She'd tucked her gun away and now had her phone in her hand, typing away.

"Updating Facebook, are we?" Eva asked.

Isabella pressed one more button then stuffed the phone in her pocket. "As a matter of fact, yes. I was updating my status: 'Just about to crash a tram, LOL'."

"Funny."

Justin had slowed, unable to keep up the pace. He appeared unaware that his pursuers were gaining on him.

The tram gradually decelerated as the traffic light ahead turned amber.

"Run the light," Eva ordered.

"But… but we will crash," the driver said, her bravado disappearing.

"You ever played video games?" Eva asked. "You have to plant your foot or you'll never get to the next level."

Instead of looking scared, the young driver's face lit up. "Like Mario Karts?"

Eva laughed. "Just like Mario Karts. If you crash, blame the chick with the gun." Eva deliberately didn't look at Isabella. She nodded at the windscreen. "Punch it."

"I've always wanted to do this!"

Eva thought the tram driver was enjoying herself a little too much. She rang the bell and leaned forward. The tram was relatively modern, but it wasn't exactly a bullet train.

The driver grabbed the microphone and practically yelled, "Stütze für Stöße!"

The passengers clutched poles and held their arms forward with panicked expressions. Isabella and Eva regarded each other in confusion.

The driver must have noticed their perplexed expressions. "I said brace for impact."

The tram didn't slow down. As the light turned red the driver clanged the bell repeatedly and bellowed a joyous squeal. She seemed to be having the time of her life.

The tram careened through the intersection and smashed into a Citroën, sending it spinning into oncoming traffic. On one side of the tram a BMW squealed to a halt and a Porsche SUV rear-ended it. On the other, two Mercedes smashed into one another. Angry drivers honked and shook their fists at the tram. But they were through.

The tram driver bounced in her seat. "I've never felt so alive!"

Eva grinned at her. "You and I should definitely hang out."

Isabella folded her arms and scowled.

Justin seemed unaware of the carnage behind him. He'd stopped and was doubled over, sucking in deep gulps of air. He didn't appear used to running. The longer he rested, the closer they got. They were a mere hundred metres away now. Even better, he had no idea they were there.

Justin was hunched near vast parkland with some sort of amusement park nearby. Eva could see the occasional flash of rides over the tree line. If they didn't catch him soon he could escape into the chaos of the park and they'd lose him. They had no time to waste.

"Let us off at the next stop." Eva didn't take her eyes off the wheezing figure ahead. "And thank you."

"Wait, wait, I can run the next set of lights!" The driver sounded hungry for more.

"That won't be necessary," Eva said evenly.

The tram driver's disappointment was palpable. It was like letting a kid go on a roller-coaster only to tell them they had to ride the merry-go-round for the rest of their life. But the driver's lust for excitement wasn't Eva's priority.

As the tram pulled up, the doors opened automatically. Eva managed to shout, "Danke!" over her shoulder as they leapt out.

With Isabella by her side, Eva threaded a path through the traffic. Justin had taken off again, but at a dawdling jog this time. He seemed spent. Eva was just getting started.

With leisurely traffic on one side of the wide street and parkland on the other, it was certainly picturesque. They were closing in on him. They had the element of surprise. They were only 20 metres away, and he had his back to them. They had him. All they needed to do was—

"'ey, Justin!"

Eva's head snapped around to stare at Isabella. *What the hell, woman?*

Their prey turned in panic and sprinted, terrified, into the park. Eva cursed and followed. She scowled at Isabella.

"What?" she asked. "We 'ave 'im."

"Not yet we don't."

Justin dashed towards the entrance of the amusement park and leapt over the barrier. An elderly security guard managed a winded, "Halt!" but nothing more.

Isabella and Eva followed suit and bounded into the park. Being late in the day, it was sparsely populated, so spotting his red shirt wasn't difficult. Cheesy music permeated the grounds, and the smell of fried food was everywhere. A giant Ferris wheel loomed over the park.

The phone in Eva's hand rang. "Volmer, we've entered an amusement park. We're close to him now."

"Keep with him. I am not far away. I shall be there with reinforcements within minutes."

Without bothering to reply, Eva hung up. Justin entered a long alleyway of arcade attractions. Eva gestured for Isabella to keep on him; she'd go the long way around and hopefully head him off. She was faster than Isabella, and Justin was exhausted.

Eva split off and sprinted past cheap amusements: quoit tossing, laughing clowns and the like. She was beginning to pant, but wasn't about to stop. Not now. She doubled down and increased her pace.

As she rounded the corner Justin spotted her. He skidded to a halt in front of the Ferris wheel, confusion and panic clear on his face. There may as well have been a bubble above his head that said, "Where the hell did you come from?"

A grin spread across Eva's face. She could see Isabella running towards him. They had him in a pincer move.

Taking a second to grab a breath, Eva said, "You have nowhere to go!"

Sweat and dread dripped from his face. With an expression of horror, Justin hurdled the barrier in front of the Ferris wheel.

"Okay, you had one place to go."

Guards yelled as Justin scrambled over the various barricades designed to corral passengers and headed directly towards the open door of an ancient carriage. Two guards leapt in front of the door, arms out, as if ready to catch him. The door closed behind them and the wheel groaned as it moved slowly upward.

Instead of backtracking, Justin sped up. He placed a foot on the barricade and launched himself into the air. Arms outstretched, he flew skyward and grabbed the ledge of the wooden carriage. The guards scrambled to seize his legs, but he managed to clamber out of their reach.

A panting Isabella reached Eva's side. Volmer and four uniformed police officers arrived seconds later. Every one of them had a gun out, spooking the tourists and guards alike.

Through halting gasps, Volmer yelled at the bemused worker manning the Ferris wheel controls. After a brief exchange, Volmer spat, "Scheisse!"

"What is it?" Eva asked.

"It has to go fully around first," Volmer explained with a scowl. After a pause, he added, "And hello. Very good pursuit, ladies."

The two agents nodded. Eva would have objected to the use of such a pejorative term, but she was too busy sucking in precious air. Volmer walked off to speak to the guards, most likely making sure they'd be ready when Justin came back down.

The phone in Isabella's pocket buzzed and she quickly glanced at it, then shoved it back in her pocket.

Eva whispered, "I'm going up there."

Isabella was stunned. "Are you mad?"

"I wish people would stop asking me that."

It was a calculated risk. Given the number of guns on the ground, Eva knew she had to calm the situation. Justin was contained, but that didn't mean the ordeal was over. When he came down there were likely to be a lot of itchy trigger fingers pointing his way. The events in Lyon had made worldwide news. People were spooked. Europe was on edge. Justin would know his options were dire. If she could talk to him she might be able to keep him from committing suicide by cop, or worse.

Eva watched the giant spinning wheel. She had to move now or she'd miss the next carriage. She didn't ask for permission—she never did. In a lightning-fast move, she bolted towards the next carriage, just as Justin had. And just like Justin, she encountered shouts, and guards trying to intercept her path.

Using the shoulder of a crouched guard as a launch pad, Eva bounded over the barricade and onto the side of the incoming carriage. It was like sprinting across stepping stones on a pond, except if she fell she wouldn't get wet—she'd fall into the churning gears of an antique mechanism. So, not quite the same.

Eva pushed herself up and rolled onto the roof. Heaving, she gazed up into Justin's astonished face, one carriage up. He gawped at her as if she was insane. As Eva glanced down at the disappearing ground, she had to concede there might be something in that.

The speed of the wheel increased—they must have been eager to get Justin back on terra firma. She didn't have long.

Over the rushing wind, she yelled, "Justin! I just want to talk. I'm unarmed."

There was a pause. "My name is not Justin Bieber!" He hid himself behind the lip of the carriage.

Eva couldn't help but smile. "I know."

"Well... good." Another pause. In a slow, tentative move, he stuck his head over the edge of the carriage. With an unwavering stare into Eva's eyes, he said solemnly, "They will kill me, you know."

"They won't." Eva shook her head. "They want to talk about the terrorist incident in Lyon. Just questions, okay?"

To Eva's utter surprise, Justin laughed. A full, unbridled belly laugh.

"Do you really think this is about terrorism?"

Her brow furrowed. "What else would it be about?"

"You... you don't know?" He tilted his head and considered her. "Oh, sweet girl, if that is true, you need to leave Europe today and never come back."

"Why would you say that?"

"Because chaos is coming. A tempest. It is coming and nobody can stop it. Not you, not me." He shook his head. "Where are you from anyway?"

"MI6," Eva replied.

"You are English."

"No I'm bloody not, mate. I'm Australian."

"Then... I do not understand." He tilted his head inquisitively. "How did you..."

"It's a long story. There were megalomaniacs, explosions, assassins and a pink umbrella. It was a whole palaver." Eva inhaled, knowing time was short. "What about you? How did you get caught up in all this?"

"Despite what the news media would have you believe, people with my skin colour are not all terrorists."

"I know that. But in my defence, your friends did blow themselves up in front of me."

"But not for terrorism. Fear isn't The Tempest's goal. There are more players at work here than you know."

"The Tempest? What do you mean The? The Tempest is actually a thing, an organization?"

Justin tilted his head. "What did you think you were chasing? A whirlwind? The Tempest will wreak devastation across this continent." He gazed at the ground. The wheel had reached its apex and begun to descend. "I do not have much time now."

Eva wondered what he was on about. If The Tempest was an organisation, of course they were terrorists. What else would they be?

"If time is running out, what do you have to lose?" she asked.

Justin knit his brow, as if contemplating the question. He rose on his knees and nodded as if permitting Eva to ask.

"If Lyon wasn't about terrorism, what was it about?"

Justin shuffled uncomfortably and pulled at his bright shirt nervously. He held Eva's gaze and took a deep gulp of air. The carriage continued to descend.

The crack was so faint Eva almost didn't hear it.

The centre of Justin's red shirt grew darker, the darkness moving outward like a stain. Dark red over bright red. He gazed at the wound, confused. Then his mouth opened in silent shock, his eyes staring pleadingly at Eva.

One second he was gawping at her, the next, Justin's limp husk toppled off the side of the carriage like a lifeless mannequin. The body fell, colliding with the spokes of the wheel on its horrific trajectory to the ground.

Eva covered her mouth as she screamed. The next minute took an eternity.

When the carriage finally neared the ground, she leapt off and landed hard. She scrambled to the body. Isabella was already there, towering over it with her pistol in hand.

Shock etched across her face. "'e 'ad a gun. I 'ad to take the shot."

Volmer approached quietly, staring at the body.

Eva wiped away a tear. "I didn't see a…"

Before Eva could finish the sentence, Isabella leaned down and rolled the body over. Clutched in Justin's lifeless hand was a small black pistol.

Eva never saw the pistol. But there it was. If he had a gun why didn't he use it to fight his way out? And why hadn't Eva seen it? She'd been so close.

The police strode up, guns ready, searching for further threats. Isabella held her pistol up, finger off the trigger, relinquishing it. One of the officers took it from her and motioned for her to follow. The police would have many questions. They weren't the only ones.

Volmer peered down at Justin's body and nudged it with his foot, as if trying to confirm that he was truly dead. He grunted.

"I did not see a gun either."

CHAPTER FIVE

"You think this is about terrorism?"

The words echoed around Eva's skull.

She sat in the BVT cafeteria on an uncomfortable aluminium chair, drinking appalling coffee from a styrofoam cup. Eva gazed out into the courtyard, where a lone anaemic tree was silhouetted in the fading light of the day. The tree seemed oddly menacing, its bare branches extended like skeletal fingers clutching at the night.

One thought occurred to her. Well, two. The first was, what else would Lyon be about if not terrorism? The second was, why hadn't the person responsible for this coffee been hung, drawn and quartered?

It was the 21st century. People blowing themselves up was, unfortunately, not that uncommon. And every single time, it had been related to terrorism of one form or another. What made Lyon any different?

There was one aspect that made Lyon stand out. No group had yet claimed to be behind the attack. That was odd, but not altogether unusual—terrorist incidents had occurred before without anyone claiming responsibility. But it still didn't sit right with Eva.

If The Tempest was an organisation, like Justin claimed, why hadn't they come out as the ones responsible? Who was behind The Tempest? What was their ultimate goal? War in Europe? Why? To what end?

In news that surprised no one, Justin's real name was not Justin Bieber. It was Nur Hakim. Born and raised in Marseille, he apparently came from a good family. Like Mustafa and the other suicide bombers, he had shown no outward signs of radicalisation. Then suddenly their photos were on every news website in the world.

To the outside world, it appeared that the incident was over. There had been a terrorist attack. The relevant government organisations had traced the perpetrators to a hotel room and found someone covering up evidence, who'd then been killed evading authorities. It was all rather neat.

Except it wasn't.

Something about it gnawed at Eva's insides. She didn't believe it was over. Not by a long shot. The maddening part was, there was little she could do about it. MI6 believed her work was done. What could a lowly new agent do to change their minds? A gut feeling was far from a persuasive argument.

But she felt sure there was more to it. For one thing, there was Justin and the gun. Eva was sure she hadn't seen one. And how had it stayed in his hand during the fall?

Another question that made her uneasy: was Isabella all she seemed? Back in the hotel room Justin had kept eyeing her. At the time, Eva had thought it was because Isabella stood between him and the door. Now she wasn't so sure.

Then again, Eva could just be paranoid. Or on some sort of bad coffee trip. Possibly both.

With their only lead dead, there was nothing more Eva could do. It wasn't like she could bundle up her doubts in a report. MI6 weren't keen on acting on "feels". Especially not from a rookie agent.

So Eva sat and drank her awful coffee because she had nothing else to do.

"'ello."

Eva glanced up. Isabella appeared ragged and drained. The French agent flopped into the seat beside her with a grunt.

"They 'ave finished my interrogation," she said meekly.

"You mean questioning?"

The DGSE agent frowned. "No, I mean it was an interrogation. They treated me like I was a 'ostile, they were incredibly aggressive."

"No idea what that's like." Eva took a sip of her coffee, more for effect than out of a desire to drink any more of the vile substance.

Isabella gave a slight pout. "Again, I am sorry about Lyon. My superiors insisted. It would 'ave been awfully unpleasant for you." She waited a moment. "Well, not all, I 'ope." She ran her thumbnail along the seam of Eva's jeans.

"Wow, you're still trying it on. Are you permanently in heat, woman?"

Isabella shrugged and lifted her eyebrows.

Eva swirled her coffee, contemplating the thoughts in her head. Not least of which was, why was the coffee grey?

"Where to from here for you?" she asked.

Isabella stretched her arms over her head. "I 'ave 'ad my weapons and phone confiscated. I will stay 'ere one night and then they will quietly put me on the first flight to France in the morning. They have made me... do you know the Latin phrasing, persona non grata? That is me."

"That's funny, because..." Eva trailed off. "Never mind."

"No, go on." Isabella nodded encouragement, seemingly happy for the distraction.

"In diplomatic relations, when someone is deemed persona non grata it's based on the Vienna Convention for Diplomatic Relations. Given where you are, you couldn't get more poignant if you tried."

It wasn't a good anecdote, but Eva needed to add something to the conversation. Isabella was being shunted out of the country as soon as possible. That meant the Austrian authorities didn't think she was completely innocent, nor completely culpable. Eva could sympathise with the sentiment.

Eva sighed. She wasn't here to play nice. "Why did you shoot him, Isabella?"

The spy pursed her lips. She wasn't upset by the question; in fact, it appeared she'd anticipated it. "Remember when I said I could never leave my partner again?" She waited for Eva to nod. "I was protecting you, Eva. I wasn't able to follow you onto that carriage, but I never took my eyes off the two of you. You are my partner, I could not leave you defenceless. I 'ad your back. There was a threat to your person, I 'ad a shot and I took it. You must believe that."

The earnestness in her answer was jarring. Perhaps the hours of questioning had worn down her defences, Eva didn't know. But in that brief instant, Eva believed every word.

Eva gazed at the tree in the courtyard. It looked less menacing than it had before. Instead of a skeletal spectre, it now appeared more like a lone outcrop of the natural world, engulfed by cold industrial surrounds.

All these doubts, but what for? Eva thought to herself. So what if the French authorities had gathered information on the terrorists suspiciously quickly? So what if Isabella was flirtatious? Bishop, an acquaintance of Eva's at MI6, was like the human equivalent of Pepé Le Pew, yet she trusted him with her life. Would she be so upset about the death of Justin if she hadn't seen him die?

"Ladies!"

Volmer strode confidently towards them. Once again, he was immaculately dressed. He beamed a broad grin at them, oozing charm, waving like they were old friends. Eva didn't buy it.

"I was hoping to take you both out for a lovely dinner this evening, but I am told that it is not to be."

"Why is that?" Eva asked.

Volmer gave a little bow. "I have been given the pleasure of escorting Madam Isabella to further questioning."

"Further?" Isabella's response was louder than it should have been. "I thought we were done."

"Alas, that is not to be. Bundesministerium für Inneres wish to ask their own series of questions. They are jackals, but while they are guests in our office they should behave themselves. I do apologise for the inconvenience. They should know never to inconvenience a lady."

Isabella ran her finger over the tabletop. "Who are these idiots? And can I have my gun back before the interview?" She paused. "Answer the second one first."

Volmer chuckled. "My apologies, the gentlemen are from the Federal Ministry of the Interior. As for your second request, I am afraid you will not see your firearm again, Fräulein. It is now evidence. The remainder of your personal effects have already been transported to your hotel room."

"If I ever get there." Isabella folded her arms.

"You will! You shall be accorded my country's supreme hospitality this evening."

"Right before you throw me out of the country," Isabella spat.

Volmer shrugged. "Let us not dwell on negatives; there are far too many in our profession, yes? Instead, let us focus on the positives."

"Such as?" Eva asked.

"The lovely sunset, the beautiful city as a backdrop, my amazing buttocks." His eyebrows danced suggestively at Eva. "All these things are worth admiring, would you not say?"

Eva tittered. "Sorry, Volmer, not going to happen."

His face fell comically. He was only half serious. "But why, my love? I had already booked the wedding chapel for myself and either or both of you."

Eva rolled her eyes. Smooth he wasn't. "Are you an emotionally abusive bad boy who will lie to me for the entirety of our relationship and in your downtime try to take over the world?"

"This seems unlikely. I do not have that much time to spare. I have just taken up Pilates."

Eva smirked. "Then you're not my type, I'm sorry."

He gave a slight shrug and turned to Isabella, his face expectant.

"You're way off." Isabella shook her head fervently. "For so many reasons."

Volmer shrugged. "You cannot blame a man for trying."

"Yes, you can." Isabella's face was etched from marble.

Volmer shrugged in defeat and bowed slightly. His phone rang and he excused himself.

As he strode away to speak in private, Eva tried to determine how she felt about Volmer. She didn't know the man, but he seemed sincere enough. The charm was forced, but there was enough genuineness in his manner to make him likeable.

"Do you want some free advice?" Isabella asked.

"Does a Humvee driver have a small penis?"

Isabella regarded Eva blankly.

"That was a yes, Isabella."

"Watch him—Volmer." It appeared Isabella was reading her mind again. "The little weasel is not as innocent as he seems."

"Why would you say that?"

"Think about it," Isabella said, watching him. "Why would the BVT assign a lone agent with no backup to that 'otel suite? Wouldn't they set up surveillance instead? You'd need that for a trial, no? Footage of a suspect rummaging around the room. Why would they allocate only one agent? Doesn't that sound all too convenient?"

Eva wanted to ask more, but it was too late. Isabella's eyes returned to the table as Volmer approached.

Isabella reluctantly pushed herself up from the table and grasped Eva's arm. "Au revoir, mon amour." She kissed Eva tenderly on the cheek.

Volmer gave a slight bow, extended his hand to Eva, kissed it, then snapped his heels together. "Goodbye. My country very much liked having you, Fräulein Eva."

Isabella leaned close enough for her warm breath to tickle Eva's ear. "And I will always regret not 'aving you."

After they left, Eva peered out into the courtyard. There were too many unanswered questions. Too many dangling threads. One thing was certain: Eva wasn't finished with the case. Not by a long shot.

Yes, she was a rookie agent, but she had brains and she intended to use them. There were so many things that didn't add up. Isabella's story about Justin and the gun was as believable as a Flat Earth convention. If Isabella deliberately took that shot, had she been acting alone?

If Justin's assassination was a deliberate act, had it been sanctioned by the DGSE? Contrary to what spy stories would have you believe, spies were not generally rogue agents, acting singlehandedly, relying on their skills and tenacity to save the day. There were dozens, if not hundreds, of dedicated professionals behind every action. If Isabella took out Justin under orders, there would be a record. But where?

Think, you stupid cow.

It took a minute of staring at the bare tree. Suddenly, Eva's mouth twisted. She remembered Isabella tapping away on her phone on the tram, joking about updating Facebook. And then she remembered Isabella received a message just before Eva leapt onto the Ferris wheel.

Isabella's phone.

If those messages were so important that Isabella would interrupt the pursuit of a suspect, Eva wanted to know what they contained. She had to get into Isabella's hotel room and steal her phone.

Eva leapt off the building.

It was lucky she was attached to a rope.

Abseiling down the outside of a ten-storey hotel in the middle of the night was a piece of cake. If that cake was laced with barbed wire and broken glass, that is. At least she liked her outfit. All black and tight Lycra. If she died, it would be in an outfit that made her butt look amazing.

Righting herself, Eva descended arse-first down the exterior of the building, very slowly. At any moment Isabella would complete her questioning and return to her room. But Eva wouldn't achieve much by plummeting to her death. A comfortable middle-ground had to be achieved.

After two floors, her pace became steady. After three she actually began to enjoy herself. She was four floors down when she became cocky and lost concentration. For a brief second Eva allowed herself to think about what she had to do when she reached Isabella's window. That moment of distraction caused her to miss the next step. Instead of brickwork, her foot met the gap where the window frame started. With her foot meeting only air, she overcompensated and completely lost her footing. Both feet slipped from the building and Eva fell.

The rope scorched her hands as she tumbled, but she couldn't let go. That would be certain death. Clasping the rope between her feet, Eva managed to slow her descent. Her fingers burned and bled, but she'd stopped the fall. She stared down at the tiny, oblivious cars driving on the street below.

Chicken punching Jesus. That was too close.

A quick count told her she was on the fifth floor. Exactly where she needed to be. Eva would have laughed if she was certain she wouldn't fall again. She didn't take the chance.

She wrapped one leg around the rope and swung herself over the centre of the window. For once, she lucked out. It slid open smoothly. Why would you lock your window five floors up? Who would be crazy enough to enter a hotel room that way? Eva had to admit it was a good question.

Eva had intended to break into Isabella's hotel room the same way they'd entered Mustafa's. Be it electronic or the old-fashioned manual method, Eva would have been in the room in seconds. At least, that was the idea. The guard stationed outside the room put a crimp in her plan.

Plan B was less appealing. Given Eva's recent experience with hotel balconies, it was a scheme she entered into reluctantly.

She'd needed equipment. Abseiling down a hotel couldn't be

done with three cocktail napkins and a complimentary bag of peanuts. She'd needed rope, and lots of it.

Unfortunately, the hotel's concierge didn't speak English or French. The ensuing pantomime as Eva requested directions to the nearest hardware store must have appeared bizarre to onlookers. She mimed using hammers, saws and lassos. Eva must have seemed like be an ultra-violent cowgirl. Eventually, the concierge caught on. After a quick taxi ride, Eva had all she needed.

It worked. Eva inelegantly tumbled into the hotel room. After what seemed like several hours, her sphincter unclenched and she let out a deep sigh of relief. As her eyes adjusted to the dark, she realised the room was a mirror of hers several floors up—that is, the same as hotel rooms the world over.

Isabella's purse and gun holster were sitting at the end of the bed. As was her phone. Eva grasped it and pressed the home button. Of course, it asked for a code or fingerprint. Eva had neither of these things.

But she would.

If a device was electronic, it could be hacked. It might take time and resources, but in this century nothing remained hidden for long. The age of secrets was over.

Eva pocketed the phone and glanced at the window, knowing the dreaded rope awaited her. But before she could take a step in that direction she heard footsteps and the sound of someone sliding in a room key.

She'd never make the window in time. The bathroom was closer. She dove in and silently closed the door behind her. Alone in the dark room, Eva could hear nothing but the thunderous sound of her own heartbeat.

The door creaked open and soft footsteps crossed the floor. There was no window in the bathroom. The shower was glass and offered no hiding place. There was no escape. Isabella would eventually need to use the bathroom. What would Eva say when that happened? There was only one thing to do.

Eva took off her clothes.

Stripped down to her underwear, she folded her pants and top in a neat pile. Eva placed her shoes on top and tucked Isabella's phone deep inside one. She blew out a silent lungful of air.

Steeling herself with a clenched fist, she opened the bathroom door. Isabella had her back to her, angrily stuffing clothes into her suitcase.

"You said you regretted not having me," Eva said in her best sultry voice. "Life is too short for regrets, wouldn't you say?"

A stunned Isabella spun around. After a moment of shock, her face lit up like a bonfire at a fireworks factory.

"I never thought we'd meet again, Eva." Her gaze rolled up and down the MI6 agent's body, lingering on her lingerie. "But I am most pleased to see you." She took a slow breath and stepped forward. "All of you."

Eva tilted her head and raised an eyebrow. Internally, she was screaming in panic. Outwardly, she channelled the ghost of Lauren Bacall. She would most likely be forced to sleep with Isabella. That's what spies did, wasn't it? Get in bed with the enemy? Did that extend to allies? At least she wouldn't have to climb that rope again.

Isabella glided towards her, positively beaming. One hand wrapped around Eva's bare waist, the other slid along her jaw. She was taking her time, admiring her unexpected gift.

Throatily, she said, "'Ow did you get into my—"

Before she could finish, the door opened and Volmer barged in, head down.

"Apologies, Fräulein Isabella, but I must ask —"

On seeing the two of them, he halted his sentence as well as his stride. It took the BVT agent a moment to assess the situation. There was Isabella, her hands on Eva, who was stripped down to her underwear.

Shock gave way to surprise, which gave way to intrigue. This in turn gave way to something else entirely. It was like all his Christmases had come at once, along with Easter, New Year's and Hanukkah. It appeared he would, too.

"Ladies, this is completely inappropriate." He shook his head for effect. "Isabella is persona non grata. My government would not stand for such fraternisation."

Volmer walked over to the hotel desk, pulled out a chair and positioned it at the end of the bed. He sat and crossed his legs.

"Should I order up some champagne?" He grinned.

Isabella took her hands off Eva and folded her arms. "We will not be performing for you, Volmer. You need to leave."

"What if you divulge critical state secrets during the throes of passion? I believe this requires close supervision." He glanced about the room. "Do you think it's possible to order some popcorn, too?"

The little man placed his feet on the bed and slid his hands behind his head. He clearly wasn't going anywhere anytime soon.

As unexpected as his entrance was, for Eva, it was entirely welcome. She couldn't speak for Isabella, but based on her scowl it seemed clear she wasn't pleased with his enforced supervision.

Eva didn't want to sleep with Isabella if she could help it. Volmer was her out.

"I can't do this with him watching!" Eva flung her hands up in exasperation. "I was already nervous." She eyed Isabella. "I'm sorry, I can't, not now."

Eva marched towards the bathroom. Volmer watched her with pleasure, clearly enjoying the show.

"Mon ange!" Isabella bellowed after her. "We can fix this, he can go!"

Eva slammed the bathroom door behind her and exhaled a huge sigh of relief. Scrambling for her clothes, she dressed to the echoing sounds of insults being flung in French and Austrian German. She tucked Isabella's phone down the back of her pants.

When Eva finally emerged, a tense détente had been reached, with both parties scowling at one another from opposite sides of the room. Eva approached Isabella and kissed her lightly on the lips. Volmer sat up.

"I'm sorry, I thought I could do this." She ran her hand down Isabella's arm. "I suppose this is finally goodbye."

The disappointment on Isabella's face was tangible. She blew out a breath, in part frustration and in part steadying herself. She extended a delicate hand.

"For the second time I am saying au revoir, Eva Destruction." She kissed her hand. "We may not meet again, but know that I will always 'ave your back."

Eva nodded and headed for the door. She couldn't look at Volmer. When she walked outside, the guard gave her a startled look, his expression an understandable *where did you come from?*

As she scurried down the hall, she reached back to confirm that Isabella's phone was still there. Relief washed over her. She tried to ignore the tiny part of her that wondered what might have been.

CHAPTER SIX

Eva lay in her hotel room and stared at the ceiling, her phone held to her ear. The TV was on mute, news coverage silently displaying endless shots of the iconic Ferris wheel.

"Hey Trev."

"Eva! This is unexpected." His enthusiasm was endearing.

Trevor was her tech guy—the one who had cracked the room key in no time. He had a crush on Eva like the bottom of the Mariana Trench. Eva didn't encourage it, or take advantage of his not-so-secret infatuation, and to his credit, Trev never let it get in the way of his work. Which is exactly why Eva was calling.

Espionage had changed. It was never all shadowy figures in trench coats and honourable, incorruptible spies, as the books would have you believe. It was more brutal, dirtier and far less moralistic than that. And in the new century it had changed again. It was less about a nation's secrets and more about protecting their citizenry from the brutality of random acts of violence.

Lyon had been a failure in that endeavour.

Espionage was still about ideologies, albeit with different end goals. The superiority of communism was no longer at stake, but some similarities survived. Although the game had changed in the new century, terrorism like communism before it, was still one group of people wanting to impose their dogma on another.

Creating fear for coercive purposes was at the root of terrorism. Lyon had achieved the fear, that much was certain. Many terrorist acts were perpetrated in the hope of prompting retaliation, making martyrs of the perpetrators and fuelling further jihad. It was this second part that was missing from Lyon.

Nobody had claimed responsibility. Not one mention of the organisation known as The Tempest. If it wasn't about making martyrs, what was it about? If it was to rejoice at how weak a country was, where was the gloating? It didn't add up.

Another changed aspect of espionage was the newfound reliance on technology. Disappearing ink and microfilm had given way to hackers and metadata. That was where Trevor came in.

"Got a job for you, Trev," Eva said. "Well, two."

"I'm all yours... I mean... um..." She could virtually feel him going red over the phone. "I mean, what can I do for you, Eva?" He let out an embarrassed sigh.

"I've sent you a mobile phone in a diplomatic pouch—you should receive it in the next few hours. I need you to crack it and search for any messages around the time of the incident at the Ferris wheel." Eva glanced up at a picture of exactly that on the TV screen.

"Oh, okay. We've made some pretty cool leaps in recent times cracking those things. Not that we'd tell the general public, of course." His earnestness was endearing. "What's the other thing?"

"Need you to do some digging for me. It's about the incident in Lyon."

"Not a problem at all," he said confidently. "Every available bod has been thrown at that, me included. So whatever you need, I'd probably be looking at it anyway."

It didn't surprise Eva in the slightest. Two cabinet ministers were dead, along with three other UK citizens. Parliament was in an uproar. The opposition were baying for the Foreign Minister's head. Eva knew her personally and was certain the minister would not go quietly. The leader of the opposition had called for an enquiry on who knew what and when. It was pure grandstanding before the next election. The findings of an espionage inquiry would never be made public, and the opposition knew that. The Prime Minister didn't have a great deal of support and the sharks could smell blood in the water.

"I'm thinking about how these kids were recruited. They're from different cities, different sects, different imams. None of them seem connected, but there they were on the same day, striking fear into the world. If this was one of those detective movies I'd be trying to join up the pieces of red string."

"You and every other agency in the world with a passing interest."

"So I'm guessing nobody's found anything?"

"As you Aussies say, bugger all mate."

His accent was actually pretty good. He'd been practising. For her. Eva decided to put that aside for now. She had to focus.

"But they were recruited, there must be breadcrumbs. They're all separate, so that means it probably wasn't in person, so that means..."

"There will be an electronic footprint of some kind. Yeah, okay, I see where you're going with this. Right, let me see what I can find. If they've found computers then they've found their digital IDs. I can start there. We'll make an IT boffin out of you yet, Eva."

"Maybe see what's on the black net too."

"The what?"

"Black... net. The thing you told me about. Where you can buy drugs and guns and stuff without being traced."

"Black...? Oh, you mean the dark web."

Eva shrugged to no one. "Sure."

Technology and Eva weren't firm friends. In her café, the point of sale was a shoebox. Computers weren't her thing. She'd been working on it, but at times she felt like one of those apes at the start of *2001: A Space Odyssey,* wailing at an obelisk.

"If it helps," Eva said, "maybe search for key word 'tempest'. Either as something bad coming or an organisation known as The Tempest. It might not show up, but you never know."

Trev promised to do his best and hung up. She knew he would. There was so much bugging her about the case, it was good to have someone who would help her work through it without thinking she was being paranoid.

She unmuted the TV. CNN was covering a live news conference. The families of the perpetrators had bravely fronted the media. Their faces were grave, full of remorse and fear. Nobody wanted their religion, their town or their family tarnished in such a way. Eva felt for them. These families, who had nothing to do with the violence, carried the burden.

Not only did they have to contend with the loss of their loved ones, but they had to endure accusations of being complicit in the acts of terror. It was a weight Eva didn't think she could take with as much grace as these people. They were brave, stoic and articulate. They were also angry. Angry at whoever had convinced their sons to perpetrate such heinous acts. Eva was going to do her best to bring these people justice.

A phone buzzed somewhere in the room. It wasn't hers—she'd spoken to Trev on that one, and it was still in her hand. It was the one Volmer had tossed her the day before.

The message simply said:

Please meet me at the Plague Column at 1 pm.
I have news regarding our mutual friend.
It seems she's been playing us all.
Come alone.
V

Eva didn't like the sound of a plague column, whatever that was. She assumed the message was from Volmer, but why send a text message and not see her in person? Why the cloak and dagger?

More questions.

Eva hoped the meeting would finally supply some answers, instead of posing more questions. There was only one way to find out. Eva was going to go see a plague column.

~

Before Eva met with Volmer, she needed to check in with her handler. With her supposed partner being thrown out of the country, Eva needed to find out where she stood.

"Hey Paul."

"Hey Evie. Still Australian?"

"Effin oath, mate. Still a pommie git?"

"The pommiest." The pleasantries out of the way, Paul leapt straight in. "I received your report and we've done some digging."

Eva had asked Paul to investigate both Isabella and Volmer. She wanted more information on who she was working with, although the former was less of an issue now.

"I'm sure it will be no surprise that spy agencies do not normally share resumes."

Eva didn't answer. She knew Paul would have something, so there was no use asking.

"However," Paul said, and Eva smirked, "it is always wise to know who your allies are."

"You spy on other spies?" Eva tsked. "I'm shocked." She really wasn't.

"Evie, this is the world's second oldest profession, we've been at this for a while. We know what we're doing."

Eva thought that sometimes it resembled the world's oldest profession, but decided not to mention that.

"They both have exemplary records. Isabella is highly skilled in," he paused as if reading, "ah, many lethal things. She'd be good to have in a scrape. There's some sort of investigation into a liaison with another operative but the details are sketchy. Apart from that, she's dreadfully highly regarded. Some say a future leader of the whole ball of wax."

That didn't surprise Eva. In their short time together Isabella had seemed extremely driven, and happy to take advantage of her station. Emptying a fancy restaurant in Lyon for a chat and a smoke was the first example that came to mind.

"But that may all be over now she's back in France," Paul continued. "The way I hear it, her political enemies are using Vienna as leverage. Politics is everywhere, I'm afraid."

"You are well informed."

Paul paused. "Spy." Eva could feel his smugness radiating through the phone. "I'll send you her file. We have some information on the midget as well."

"Pretty sure you can't say 'midget', Paul."

"Can't I? It's so hard to keep up with what's politically correct."

"You'll find 'midget' is highly offensive to those with dwarfism. I think the States prefer 'Little People', but 'person with dwarfism' is accepted everywhere else. Ideally, you just call them by their name."

"How are you so knowledgeable about such things?"

"It's called Google, dude."

"Ah, I've heard of that," he said dryly. "Anyway, he checks out, too. Although apparently he has a temper, so that's probably why he's not higher up."

"Is that a short joke?"

"It is now."

Eva told him about the mysterious text from Volmer. Paul being Paul, he already knew Isabella's phone was on its way to Trevor.

He cleared his throat. "How did you get her phone, Eva?"

"Ah, I was hanging around and there it was."

"Right." His tone made it clear he didn't believe a word of it. "Evie, you need to stop being so reckless. Leaping off balconies, jumping on Ferris wheels, these are not the actions of an MI6 agent who still wants to have a job by Christmas." There was an earnestness in his voice Eva found unsettling. "I'm going to be honest. I'm getting all sorts of pressure to recall you. You're a rookie agent on her own. They're saying you shouldn't be running around Europe creating headlines."

"What should I be doing? Staying in the office and making them coffee?"

"Now, Evie, that's not..."

"Look Paul, I know I've stuffed up. Both Lyon and Justin could have been handled better."

"Who?"

"Nur Hakim. I know I'm a fresh agent, Paul, I get that, but there's something going on here that's not normal."

"That's the problem, Evie. You're fresh out of the packet, and they're asking how you know what normal is. Espionage is a weird beast, it's not what they show you on the telly."

He had a good point, but Eva wasn't about to concede.

"Do you think I'm good at my job? Do I give absolutely everything to what I do?"

"Without a doubt in the world," he said firmly. "I've tasted your coffee." He gave a little chuckle; he was deescalating the discussion. "And I've never known anyone with better instincts, either." He sighed. "Go do what you do, Evie. I'll protect you as best I can, but you need to work fast, alright? I can only distract them with shiny things for so long."

"Understood."

Eva rang off and stared at the ceiling. No pressure, then. All she had to do was find evidence to back up her vague feelings, and potentially outsmart professionals who had been in this game far longer than she had—all within the next day or so.

Piece of cake.

The only trouble was, that cake seemed to be in a heavily guarded steel vault, buried deep underground.

On the moon.

~

To Eva's surprise the Plague Column was not a euphemism. It was an actual column of plague.

Well, at least an artistic representation of such. The sculpture was carved in a twisted, swirling statue full of crazy-looking characters, mad kings and snarling beasts. It was located on the beautiful Graben strip of high-end shops, taking centre stage in the wide, car-free mall.

Eva couldn't seem to take her eyes off it. Every angle of the sculpture offered something new.

"It is beautiful, yes?"

Eva turned to see Volmer standing beside her, admiring the monument.

She nodded. "And horrific."

Volmer pursed his lips in agreement. "In my experience these two things are usually intertwined."

Eva didn't reply. Instead, she sat at the base of the statue and motioned for Volmer to join her. He parked himself with a plop and glanced back at the plague column.

"It is one of the great ironies of the city," Volmer said, mostly to himself. "It was made to commemorate the last great plague. The Kaiser promised to erect it if his people were saved."

"Noble, I guess." Eva shielded her eyes from the light reflecting off the gold of the statue.

"Oh, he was most noble," Volmer said, dripping with insincerity. "Leopold the First fled the plague as soon as it arrived, leaving the people to fend for themselves."

"Ah."

Volmer grinned, pleased Eva had gotten his point. "This is the way of great men, would you not say? Sending innocents to their deaths while they sleep soundly on sheets of silk."

"You're quite philosophical today."

"It is Tuesday. I am very philosophical on a Tuesday," he said earnestly. "On Wednesdays I speak only in haiku."

"And Thursdays?"

"I rap in Yiddish."

Eva giggled. He certainly did have charm.

"Why am I here, Volmer?"

"My scintillating company?"

"That's a given." Eva smiled. "But apart from that?"

Volmer's face suddenly turned serious. The transition was unsettling. One second he was all charm, the next he looked grave, practically scared.

"How well do you know Isabella?"

"Not well at all. Only a few days, since the attacks in Lyon."

Eva imagined her partner was back in France by now, safely

within the confines of her own home. She wondered how Isabella's superiors would respond to her actions in Vienna.

He tilted his head. "You seemed rather intimate last night."

"Well, yes, ah. That was a once-off, I assure you."

"Very well, that is your business, of course. But I need to know how close you are with that woman."

"Not exceptionally. The first time we met she tied me up."

"I do not need to hear your sexy talk. At least not without a stiff drink in front of me."

"No, not like that..." Eva closed her eyes to compose herself. "What is this about, Volmer? Is this concerning the incident at the Ferris wheel? Because I have my own doubts about that."

"Oh, as do I, pretty lady, as do I."

Eva's feminist hackles immediately went up, but now was not the time to smash the patriarchy.

Volmer went on. "But there is more to it than that, I assure you. So much more."

"Like?"

"She had an ex-lover, a spy, like the both of you."

"The one who was killed? She told me."

"She did?" He sat up straight. "Then you also know her ex-lover is not dead. Why doesn't MI6 have every available agent on this?"

"What? Wait up." Eva held up her palms. "Isabella's ex is alive? Alexis is alive?"

Confusion crossed Volmer's face. "Alexis? You mean—"

Volmer never finished the sentence. His head splintered in an explosion of skull fragments and blood.

CHAPTER SEVEN

Screams filled Graben as well-dressed locals and tourists alike shrieked in panic. One second Volmer was casually chatting, the next his head had been blown apart by an unseen bullet.

Shoppers scrambled over one another, running in all directions. Not knowing where the shooter was meant nowhere was safe. Eva dove to the ground and rolled. She extracted her pistol and lunged at the opposite side of the column.

Further bullets pummelled the statue, splintering wood, plaster and marble. The gunshots echoed around the canyon of buildings. Any pedestrians not already alerted by the first bullet stampeded at the further salvos. Europe was a continent on edge; it needed little encouragement.

Weapon facing skyward, safety off, Eva assessed her situation. Volmer's wound was so complete, so devastating, it could only have come from a high-calibre weapon. That meant a sniper. That meant Eva wasn't safe even behind the base of the column.

She didn't glance back at Volmer's body. She couldn't. She'd liked the short-statured man. He was charming and funny. But now he was dead. Eva's survival instinct took over. She would mourn later, but first she had to avoid dying the same way he had.

The statue only afforded temporary cover. With panicked pedestrians fleeing the street, she had no chance of blending into the crowd. While the bullets had stopped temporarily, that was only because she'd found brief cover. She'd have to come out eventually. If the sniper was well-hidden and patient enough, she would be an easy target. Worse, if there was more than one shooter, she was screwed.

Eva needed to even the odds.

Making a mental map of the square, there were countless sniper nest options. High buildings on all sides with plenty of windows provided ample spots to set up a rifle. But the sniper would need the ability to get away cleanly. On a pedestrian strip, that wasn't so easy. Plus, the buildings were old—not all the windows opened.

Think.

She thought back to her phone conversation with Paul. He'd called her reckless. He was right. She'd been far too impulsive. She'd chased down a suicide bomber, spent all her ammunition and practically told him he had loose wires. She *was* reckless. She needed to do better. She needed to *be* better.

Eva could either keep making the same mistakes or learn from them. She needed to live up to Paul's expectations. She needed to become an MI6 agent. *Time to grow the hell up, Princess.*

The sniper would have to be elevated in order to get a clean shot. They couldn't shoot through a crowd, they would need to be above it. Eva pulled out her phone and put it in enhanced photo mode, then held the camera over the base of the statue. She scanned for open windows or the barrel of a gun poking over a building ledge. There were only a finite number of positions from which that shot could have been taken. She also took into account access to cross streets and light rail stations for getaway options.

Painstaking minutes later, Eva had the bastard. He wasn't in a building at all. He lay atop a souvenir kiosk further down the street. There he was, face down, grey hoodie on, peering through his sniper scope. It was a good position. Slightly raised, invisible to passers-by, easy access to the street when he was done. It was perfect—until Eva spotted him. He was no longer a sniper now. He was prey.

Mental calculations were made, tactics formed. She was armed; always a bonus. But her adversary had a scope, and better range. Nothing was to be gained by further contemplation. Eva had to act. She took off her sweater.

Eva exhaled. She'd have one chance, then the element of surprise would be blown. She steeled herself with one great inhale.

Let's do this, you wazcock.

Eva threw the sweater to her left and instantly moved to her right. In seconds, her top was peppered with bullets. Eva commenced firing at the souvenir kiosk as she ran towards it. She counted her shots as she sprinted. *Eight, seven, six.* The sniper ducked for cover. *Five, four, three.* Eva kept firing, her aim true. *Two, one.*

She dove into the open doors of a department store. She'd gained 20 metres. Not bad. But it was less than halfway, and now she'd lost the element of surprise. Eva reloaded.

The department store had been her goal all along. The store was large and had more than one entrance onto Graben. The sniper had missed his best chance of taking Eva out. Now she had the advantage, and he was cornered.

Eva ran through the department store, gun in hand. Racks of fancy clothes and half-dressed mannequins flashed by. She screamed for people to move out of her way. Frightened pedestrians who had sought safety in the store did exactly that. The angry armed woman always had right of way.

By now, she was sure the sniper would be panicked. Either his quarry had eluded him or she was coming after him. Neither option was great, but if he was wise he would fear Eva's wrath.

Nearing the second entrance, she slowed. Unfortunately it didn't offer a clear eyeline to the kiosk, but it did afford other benefits. The sniper couldn't know she would emerge from that entrance. If he was a good strategist, he'd suspect it, but he'd never know for sure. That gave Eva an advantage. One she was ready to exploit.

With her gun in her hands and a full clip loaded, Eva was as prepared as she was ever going to be. She gritted her teeth and cracked her neck.

With a banshee-like screech, Eva tore through the entrance, firing her pistol at the roof of the kiosk. She was relentless in her shots, not giving the sniper a chance to return fire. At close range his rifle would be more of a hindrance.

She ejected the clip and threw it aside, slapping in another. She pulled back the slide and fired once again. Still no response.

In the last 2 metres before she reached the kiosk, Eva took giant strides and launched herself. She clambered up the side, holding on to the roof with one hand, pistol in the other. She flung her arm over the roof and hauled herself up, ready to blow away the man who killed Volmer and tried to assassinate her.

There was nothing on the roof but a sniper's rifle. A lone Remington 700, still positioned on its bipod. The sniper had fled. Eva thumped her fist on the roof.

"Twatfaced fucknuggets!"

She scanned the virtually empty street. At the nearest cross street, a lone grey-hooded figure jumped on a red Ducati motorbike. He plunged in the key and threw a panicked glance over his shoulder. The fear in his eyes told her all she needed to know. He knew she was on his arse.

Eva jumped off the roof. With feet firmly planted on the sidewalk, she stared the sniper down.

With shaking hands, he started the engine.

Eva raised her pistol.

He pulled the clutch and tapped his foot to put the bike in gear.

Eva cracked her neck.

The bike spun its wheel and he fishtailed off.

Eva exhaled.

He wove through pedestrians.

Eva closed one eye and aimed.

The bike dipped off the curb and sped down the road.

Eva fired.

The front tyre exploded and an instant later the bike slid out from beneath the sniper. Sprawling over the handlebars, he landed heavily on his back and slid along the asphalt into the path of oncoming traffic. A Mercedes skidded to a halt mere centimetres from the sniper's head.

Scrambling to his feet, the sniper sprinted away from Eva, who gave chase. The tables had turned, and Eva didn't want them to turn any further. She made ground quickly.

The side street was just as empty as Graben. The lone figure was an easy mark. Her prey didn't look back once, so intent was he on his mad scramble for freedom. He tore at his hood and ripped it off his head.

He was only a kid. His white, bare skull was adorned with random amateurish tattoos. His movements were erratic, betraying his fear. He should be afraid. Moments before he had been a god with power over life and death. Mere seconds later, he was bolting for his life.

She had a clean shot. Centre mass, easy kill. She could take him. No collateral damage. One shot and he'd be down.

Eva didn't take it.

Sprinting after him, she had another plan. It wasn't reckless. Crossing the road, she passed a sparsely populated café near a Louis Vuitton store. A lady's blue coat hung over the back of a chair. Without breaking stride, Eva stole the coat and kept running.

She wished she had her surveillance pack. It would have made shadowing the kid so much easier. Unfortunately, it was tucked away in the hotel room, no use to her whatsoever.

The young sniper made a beeline for the train station. Eva knew Karlsplatz Station was a central hub, just as she knew she couldn't let him slip through her fingers.

The kid never glanced over his shoulder. He dashed down the escalators, weaving through commuters as he descended towards the station. He must have thought he'd lost her.

Good luck with that, Twatmonkey.

He barrelled through the touch-on point and sprinted towards the platform, where the clatter of an oncoming train assaulted Eva's ears. She walked towards the platform and slipped on the coat. As she stood waiting for the train, she did her best to appear inconspicuous while sucking in lungfuls of air.

Extracting the hair tie from her ponytail, she shook her dark hair loose. Anything to mask her identity. She used the reflection in the glass of a nearby advertisement to keep her prey in view. Hiding behind a group of backpackers, Eva tried to gather her thoughts.

What the hell is this all about?

Eva assumed whatever Volmer had been trying to tell her had gotten him killed. That meant someone knew what he knew, and they knew Volmer was about to tell Eva. But what was it?

Passengers shuffled in readiness as the train approached. The sniper was so focused on getting onboard that he ploughed through the alighting passengers, never once observing his surroundings. Eva followed, careful to keep other commuters between her and her target. The train left the station and she used the reflection in the windows to make sure he stayed put.

As she listened to the soothing *clickety clack* of the train, Eva returned to her musings. What was the critical information Volmer had been trying to give her? Eva ran through the conversation in her head. What had Volmer said? That Isabella's former lover was alive. Why did the name Alexis surprise him? And why did he specifically say that MI6 should have agents searching for her? Surely that was DGSE's problem?

For several minutes, questions bounced around Eva's brain, but no answers shook loose. It was like doing a jigsaw puzzle in the dark, while wearing boxing gloves and someone was playing a tuba. Eva hated the tuba. She needed more information. She needed the sniper, and she needed to know who had sent him.

The train slowed and the sniper rose from his seat. Trying to appear as casual as possible, he shuffled towards the door. Eva didn't buy it. If his jaw was any more clenched it would snap. Thankfully, other commuters were using the same stop, so Eva waited for them to walk along the aisle before she stood up.

The train came to a halt and the doors slid open. The signs said Längenfeldgasse Station. The sniper bolted towards the exit, and

Eva pushed past passengers and did the same. She wasn't about to lose him now.

He sprinted up the escalators, weaving around chatting travellers. Eva followed, keeping enough distance between them that he wouldn't notice her pursuit. She tried to recall all her training and all the books she'd read on street surveillance. Sometimes having a near-photographic memory came in handy.

He didn't seem to suspect he was being followed. He never looked around, never doubled back or altered his course. He was certainly in a hurry.

Where are you going, little man?

He rushed out of the station and across a cobblestoned street. Head down, hoodie back over his head, he plodded towards a stone bridge over a small river. Graffiti adorned the buildings, and the area appeared more run-down than other parts of the city Eva had seen.

The sky grew darker. It was late in the day, but a storm also appeared to be brewing. Low clouds seemed ready to break at any moment, giving the city an ominous haze.

Once over the bridge, the sniper turned left and crossed the street. He certainly had a destination in mind. He slowed as he approached a darkened hotel. The weathered red sign stated it was the "Star Inn Hotel"—or at least, it had been. The windows were boarded up, and graffiti and rubbish littered its exterior. It didn't appear to have been operating for some time. A curved, paved driveway rose up to meet a portico at the front.

Suddenly the heavens opened up, and sheets of rain fell. The sniper seemed oblivious. He trudged up the driveway, hands in pockets, rain soaking his hoodie. A late-model Peugeot idled in the abandoned driveway. He went directly to the driver's window and started talking. The driver was obscured by the street lights bouncing off the windscreen. Eva held back, observing from afar.

A leather-gloved hand extended from the driver's side window and handed the rain-soaked shooter a package. It was large enough to be a bundle of cash.

The shooter accepted the package with a nod and turned to

walk away, then hesitated. He took a step towards the blue car and appeared to try and explain something, using hand gestures. One motion appeared to be that of a rifle, followed by a shake of the head. The sniper talked rapidly, as if trying to justify himself. He raised both hands, as if to say *not my fault*.

Eva heard raised voices. An accusatory gloved finger stabbed out of the car. The sniper, for his part, seemed to be giving back as good as he got. Gestures became more animated, voices rose.

Until the gunshot.

The sniper was propelled backwards, as if punched by an invisible fist. He collapsed onto the driveway and didn't move. Nothing happened for several seconds. Perhaps the driver was making sure the sniper was actually dead. Then, slowly, the car edged its way down the dark driveway.

Eva sought cover on the soggy street. The car crept towards her, then stopped. Brake lights lit up the exterior of the hotel, then the car reversed up the driveway. As it neared the body, the Peugeot stopped and the door opened. A gloved hand reached out and picked up the package that had been given to the sniper. The door slammed and the car moved back down the driveway.

Eva held her gun by her side, ready to act. Things were unravelling quickly, she needed to keep up. So much death, so much at stake. She flicked off the safety.

As the car drew close to Eva's position, she casually stepped into the Peugeot's path. The rain pelted her, the headlights shone in her eyes. She raised her pistol. The car stopped.

Now what? Eva thought to herself.

Rain cascaded down the windscreen, obscuring the driver, but Eva didn't need a clear view to know where the driver sat. She pulled back the hammer as water bounced off the barrel of her gun.

"Get out of the car." She aimed at the driver's side. "Now."

There was no response except for the low *thrum* of the car's engine.

Eva thought of issuing her command in different languages, but didn't see the point. Someone aiming a gun at your head generally sent a clear message as to what your next move needed to be.

Eva lost her patience. The driver's side mirror exploded in plastic and glass. She pulled the hammer back again. Rain continued to fall. The car continued to thrum. Eva aimed at the driver's side of the windscreen. She remained silent. The driver knew what she wanted.

The two forces faced off for several moments. The only sounds were the quiet purr of the engine, the constant rain and the faint sound of distant traffic.

Eva shot the second side mirror, its obliteration as comprehensive as the first. As Eva retargeted, the engine roared and the car jerked forward. She fired at the driver, punching holes in the windscreen. The car barrelled forward. Eva kept firing. There was no chance to dive out of the way.

Eva tucked her forehead into the crook of her elbow and placed her palms on the back of her head. The head had to be protected, she'd read somewhere. She leapt up as the car tore towards her. As it hit, she rolled, keeping her back to the glass and her head tucked between her elbows.

Tumbling end over end, gravity lost all meaning. Every part of her was pummelled, the wind knocked out of her and pain smashed into her. She bounced over the roof of the car, then she was in mid-air. Eva didn't know if she was up or down. She hung there for what seemed like eons, then gravity decided to show her precisely which way was down. She landed on her back with a thud, knocking any remaining air from her lungs.

The car screeched down the road. Pistol still clenched in her grip, Eva groaned and raised her arm. Blood dripped into her left eye, but she was alive. That meant she could fight. She blasted the rear window of the Peugeot, letting them know they'd failed, and that Eva Destruction would make them pay.

Eva loosed two more shots, but it was too late, they had escaped.

Eva spat blood and struggled to her feet. Hands moved over

her body, checking for broken bones. Everything appeared in place. Except maybe her pride.

But Eva knew how to find the driver.

It had only been a glimpse, that was all she needed. Right before she'd tumbled over the roof of the car, the light had fallen on the driver's face.

She knew who had killed the sniper. That meant she knew who'd hired him. She knew who'd had Volmer killed.

Eva had seen her face.

Isabella.

CHAPTER EIGHT

"I bloody well knew it, Paul!"

Eva held the phone to her ear and paced the hotel room like a caged panther. A particularly angry and rabid caged panther. And an armed one at that.

She should have followed her instincts. Isabella couldn't be trusted. The whole flirting thing was a distraction. The woman had a plan all along.

When Eva had contacted Paul in a rage after being struck by the car, he'd insisted she go to hospital. They'd patched her up and confirmed nothing was broken, though the bruises were coming thick and fast. She was turning so purple people would soon confuse her for Grimace.

After returning to her hotel, Eva wanted to call Paul back immediately but there was one thing she had to do first. She'd shut the blinds, turned off her phone and put a "Do Not Disturb" sign on her door. Eva remembered Ludger Volmer. The funny, charming man. His words may have veered into chauvinism occasionally, but he'd seemed to be coming from a good place. And then he was assassinated, right beside to her. Eva squatted with her back to the wall and let the regret wash over her. She hadn't known him long enough for tears, but she owed him that and more. She owed him revenge.

When she'd called Paul he'd told her what she already knew. The Vienna police had confirmed that the prints on the sniper rifle matched the kid Eva had pursued and seen murdered. At least the authorities believed that much. The other part of the story was more difficult for them to accept as true.

After lengthy questioning by the local police and the BVT, Eva had been released. After the story she'd told, she would have thought Isabella would be the most wanted woman in Austria, but that wasn't the case. The police and BVT didn't believe Eva could have identified Isabella while flying over the windscreen. They took her statement with a huge serving of scepticism.

All borders were on alert, but Eva didn't think that would be much use. Isabella was far too clever to be caught that way. The DGSE had been informed, but Paul had said they were yet to respond to Eva's accusations.

Eva knew what she'd seen. It was Isabella. She'd killed Justin at the Ferris wheel. She'd hired a killer to murder Volmer, and probably Eva too. When that was botched, she'd executed the sniper.

It was no longer a collection of vague suspicions, Eva had seen Isabella killing in cold blood. She was meant to be in France. Isabella had shot straight to number one on MI6's "If-you-wouldn't-mind-could-we-possibly-have-a-chat?" list.

Now the obvious question: why?

That was exactly what Paul and Eva were currently trying to work out, but they were coming up empty.

"Oh, and another thing," Paul said, interrupting Eva's thoughts. "When I contacted the DGSE, they claimed to have no record of your interrogation with Isabella."

"What? Does that mean she was operating independently?"

"Possibly, or it could mean they're covering their arses because the faeces has just hit the electric cooling apparatus."

The more Eva learned about this case, the less it made sense. Why would a DGSE agent be involved in terrorist acts? Why would Isabella deliberately take down a suspect, then target agents from other agencies? Eva needed more pieces of the puzzle.

She sighed. "So we don't know if she was acting under orders or had gone rogue."

"Not definitively, but we do know she wasn't acting alone. The phone you sent to Trev? He cracked it."

"Finally, some good news. What did he find?"

A small chuckle from Paul. "Exactly what you thought he would. Isabella messaged at four fifty-four in the afternoon, right about the time you said you were on the tram. She sent a message asking if she should take out the 'final obstacle'."

Eva clenched her fist. "And she received a reply?"

"Yes, four minutes later, a one-word reply: 'proceed'."

That must have been when Eva was at the base of the Ferris wheel, about to jump on. Well, that confirmed Isabella had at least one accomplice. She'd been given the go-ahead to shoot Justin when she had the chance.

"We traced the number but unfortunately that's where our luck runs out. It was a disposable phone, paid for in cash at a convenience store in Slovakia. I doubt we're going to find much there. It's since been deactivated." Paul sipped something, most likely tea. Sometimes the Englishman could be such a cliché. "Trev mentioned you also asked him to look into how the terrorists were recruited on the dark web? Any videos mentioning tempest and the like?"

Eva had nearly forgotten about that. Luckily her crew hadn't.

Paul went on. "He found a few. We traced them back to IPs in Austria and France. There is mention of an oncoming tempest, as well as a war in Europe. The organisation behind it also calls themselves The Tempest. Pretty damn ominous stuff. We have the IT boffins working to see if they can narrow in on who The Tempest actually are or at least where exactly they're posting these videos from."

"Hmm," Eva was only half listening. "Paul, I need you to do me a favour."

"No, Evie, I can't do it."

"I haven't even asked."

"You don't need to. I can read you like a neon billboard, woman."

Eva pursed her lips. "I need you to get me on the first flight to Paris."

"I'm afraid I can't do that Evie."

Her fist clenched the phone so hard she was afraid it would break. "Why?"

"The hammer is down, I'm afraid. Top brass has made the call. You're being recalled immediately. You instigated an unauthorised pursuit in which you failed to apprehend the suspect and he ended up dead, again. And then you failed to detain *his* killer, I hate to sound glib, but that's the way they're reading it upstairs."

Eva knew Paul was in a tough position. On one hand, he was one of her very best friends in the world. On the other, he was a professional. He had to follow the correct protocols. But at that precise moment, Eva didn't give a flying fig.

Paul went on. "I warned you, didn't I? This had all eyes on it, on you. I know that isn't how it all went down, mind, but that's how it's being spun. The upshot is, my love, you're being benched until an internal inquiry has been conducted. And based on who is pushing this through, I think you're in trouble. I don't to sound alarmist, Evie, but to be perfectly frank, you'll be damn lucky to have a job at the end of all this."

That was it then? Eva had worked barista jobs that lasted longer than her career with MI6.

"Then you're saying I have nothing to lose?"

A pause. One of Paul's famous pauses. "No, I'm not saying that at all." His words tumbled out fast. "Evie, I know what you're implying here. If you are facing disciplinary action and likely dismissal from MI6, then what's the point in playing by the rules? That's what you're thinking, isn't it?"

Eva shrugged. "Not at all," she lied. "Anyway, on an unrelated topic, I think I need some time off, Paul."

"Okay." His voice was wary. "When you come back, I'll make sure you get some paid leave after we—"

"Now. I need some time off now. For personal reasons."

"Evie, we both know what you're planning, and it is my duty to inform you that you're swinging awfully close to a word that starts with t and ends in reason. Don't follow her back to France."

"Paul, she killed Volmer." Eva hoped he didn't hear her growl. "And she hit me with a car."

"Yes, I understand, but you need to realise—"

"Paul," Eva strained to keep her voice under control. "She. Hit. Me. With. A. Fucking. Car. I want blood."

"You need to keep that anger in check, Evie."

"With a car, Paul!"

"Calm down."

"I will," she sighed. "I will." Eva took a deep breath. "After I punch her in the crotch. Like, a lot."

"Evie…"

"And really hard, too. I'll take a run-up and everything."

"I'm going to be explicitly clear here, so there's no chance of miscommunication. Do not, under any circumstances, go to France. Do you hear me? Evie? Don't go to France."

The "fasten your seatbelts" sign pinged off and passengers unbuckled their straps. Overhead bins were flung open and people scrambled for position, eager to be first off the plane.

Eva unclipped her belt and gazed out the window. Her brief tenure at MI6 was probably over. She was going to miss it.

She'd been hired over the cries of older, more dignified white men who claimed she'd be a disruptive influence. That, argued Paul and Bishop, was precisely why she should be hired. Eva thought differently to other spies, had different life experiences, and attacked problems in unique ways. She had game, too. She'd brought down a megalomaniac hell-bent on manipulating the world to his own ends. She'd been damn good at it, too. Now, after a year of training, it seemed it had all been for nothing. Eva hadn't saved the world this time. She couldn't even save an abhorrent sniper. Maybe she wasn't cut out for this gig. Maybe those old stuffed shirts at MI6 had been right all along. Tattoos and attitude meant little in the face of real-world espionage. She'd go back to where she did her best work: making coffee.

But there was one thing she needed to do before ending her career as a spy.

Catch another spy.

Over the loudspeaker, the pilot said, "Bonjour ladies and gentlemen, welcome to Paris."

She retrieved her bag from the overhead bin and shuffled towards the exit. With her castle in the Rhone Valley, she was practically a local. French immigration should probably know her on sight by now. That was part of the problem. She was travelling under a burn identity, one she'd use once and dispense with. She couldn't risk Isabella knowing she was coming.

That is, if she was even in the country. Would Isabella be stupid enough to return to the DGSE? Paul mentioned they were noncommittal regarding their agent's alleged actions. Perhaps they were waiting to talk to her themselves. Or maybe she'd been acting under orders. Either way, Eva would meet Isabella again.

Eva proceeded to the airport exit. Austria and France being part of the Schengen Area meant Eva didn't have to worry about customs, but she was flying under the name of Lea Ackland anyway, just to be safe. Not as inventive as Chlamydia Phlegm, but it would do the job.

Theoretically, Isabella could be anywhere on the continent—or in the world for that matter. But Eva didn't think so.

She got into a taxi and gave the driver an address.

She knew where to start.

Eva recalled the conversation she'd had with Isabella. "A little café, overlooking a park near my parents' 'ome in Créteil. It always made me feel protected, like a womb, yes?"

Except that was a lie too. She didn't grow up in Créteil. She grew up in Saint-Blaise. Eva had her file. There was one park near her parents' old home, and there was an old café there still operating. It made sense for Eva to camp out there. Well, it made only a little sense, but it was all Eva had.

If it was any more of a long shot Eva would have been on Mars. Eva had staked out the café for two days, living off eclairs, tarts and brioche. She was certain she was turning into a pastry. But this was where her gut told her to be. Eva had no other choice, unless you counted a full-frontal assault on DGSE headquarters, and that probably wouldn't end well.

The café was small and cosy, and the elderly proprietors were warm and welcoming. If these were the people Isabella had sought sanctuary with as a child, Eva could understand why. They knew everyone by name, asked about their families and shared jokes like old friends. The worn wood of the tables, the smells of home cooking, the warm family atmosphere was intoxicating. Eva wanted to stay here herself. Although after two days, the owners were giving the odd tattooed foreigner suspicious glances.

Nearing closing time on the second day, Eva conceded the folly of her choice. Surely Isabella would have a bolthole somewhere else in the world. Eva did. In a little town in Australia she had a house, fully paid up. Inside were currencies of all descriptions, hidden gold and silver bars, false identities and a weapons stash— her insurance policy. She was certain Isabella would have something similar. Most spies would, just in case their profession turned on them.

The bell above the door gave an anaemic *tung*, having lost its crisp *ting* long ago. A woman in large dark sunglasses strode in. She wore an equally large black hat, blonde hair poking out like albino spider legs. There was something familiar in her walk.

Behind the counter, the owner gave a half smile and a hesitant nod, as if she wasn't sure if she recognised the woman or not. The woman briefly scanned the café and ordered half a dozen batards. The owner wrapped them in paper and seemed on the verge of asking something, but before she had the chance, the newcomer handed over some cash. With a curt, "Merci" she rushed out the door and onto the street.

Eva watched the woman leave. Her mannerisms had a familiarity to them. Sure, the hair was different, and the clothes gave the impression of a larger woman. Even her body movements had a stiffness to them, but there was no denying it. It was Isabella.

Eva flung a fistful of Euros on the table and she was off. She considered calling Paul, but what would she tell him? "Oh, hey, disobeyed your direct order, but I found her, send help!" Even if MI6 were on her side, the apprehension of a DGSE agent on French soil would be a diplomatic minefield. No, Eva was on her own. On Isabella's home turf. With no backup. Or plan.

What the hell are you doing, Eva?

In a flash, the answer came to her: *your job*. It was a surprise, even to her. The answer was simple enough, but the implications were huge.

Eva wanted to be an MI6 agent. She enjoyed it. And she was damn good at it, despite her past mistakes, and the opinions of others. This was her life now, and she wanted to keep it that way.

Eva exited the café, her own disguise an exercise in minimalism. Baggy long-sleeved top, aviator glasses and hair tied up in in a ponytail, tucked under a baseball cap. It wasn't what you would call a master disguise, but Eva had hoped it would have afforded her at least a moment of obscurity. But the way Isabella had shot out of the café, Eva knew she'd been made. Time for a new tactic.

Saint-Blaise must have been a quaint part of Paris once. Now decidedly rundown, this area appeared dominated by those who cared little for the old ways. Older dusty cars, piles of litter and roaming wild dogs on the streets. The quaint little café seemed to be the last bastion of the old guard, slowly surrendering to a less caring world.

Isabella would know she'd been made, too. The DGSE agent would be well-versed in street counter-surveillance. Eva needed to act quickly. Right now Isabella was probably doubling back, performing blind turns, utilising her knowledge of the local streets. That was old-school espionage. Eva's solution was anything but.

Remaining completely stationary, Eva activated an app on her phone. It only took a minute. The screen showed Isabella walking down a street, totally oblivious to the fact she was being watched. She was performing all the right moves: stopping randomly to apparently tie her shoe, utilising cross streets to innocuously peer behind her. The longer Eva watched, the more casual Isabella's stride became.

She had no idea she was being followed. Fifty metres above the streets of Saint-Blaise a microdrone tailed Isabella. The unpiloted aerial vehicle, or UAV, kept pace with ease. The drone was equipped with high-definition cameras and infrared thermal imaging capabilities, and its intelligence software used facial recognition and clothing detection. Once Eva tapped on her, the drone locked onto Isabella and shadowed her every move.

It was the only bit of tech Eva actually liked using. Her instructor had called it Eva-proof equipment. Modern technology wasn't her friend, but as this was almost completely hands-off, it was a pleasure to use. Once she'd identified Isabella, the drone did everything else.

As she walked towards Isabella's location Eva felt no need to rush. The drone did the hard work; all she had to do was wait for Isabella to reach her destination. On screen, Isabella strode unhurriedly towards a block of flats. They appeared decidedly rundown and low-rent. The perfect hiding place. Unless you were being followed by a surveillance drone, that is.

Isabella unlocked the front door of the apartment block and went in. Eva didn't know which apartment she was hiding out in, but there appeared to be only half a dozen in total, judging by the doorbells at the entrance. She'd narrowed the search from the entire world to a handful of apartments. Not a bad afternoon's work.

There was a spring in Eva's step as she strode in Isabella's direction. With any luck, she'd have her apprehended by the end of the day. Just as Eva reached peak smugness, Isabella appeared on Eva's screen.

She'd emerged on the balcony of one of the apartments and

was staring directly into the drone's camera. In one smooth movement Isabella raised a gun and shot the drone. Eva's screen went black.

She'd been made.

Stupid wazcocking technology.

Eva broke into a run. Isabella knew she was coming. She was armed. She was cornered. She'd be ready for Eva.

Not that any of that mattered. Eva hadn't come this far to lose Isabella now.

As she sprinted around the final corner, Eva pulled out her pistol. The time for stealth was over. It was time to make some noise.

Without breaking stride, Eva bounded up the stairs and shouldered the cheap wooden front door. It splintered from its hinges as Eva burst through. She scanned the hallway: no threats present. Above her was a glass atrium, the once-transparent glass milky with age, moss growing where there had once been a clear view of the sky.

Her gun raised, she moved up the stained, aged stairs. They creaked underfoot, sounding like bass drums to Eva.

Her pistol sweeping left to right, she edged along the mildewy hallway. A cacophony of exotic smells seeped from under the apartment doors. The faint sounds of TVs and radios added to the soundscape. There was no way Eva would hear Isabella coming. The counter was that she wouldn't hear Eva, either.

She paused at the door of the apartment where Isabella had fired on the drone. The longer she hesitated, the more time the DGSE agent would have to escape. Eva couldn't let that happen. Using her heel, she kicked the door in. Just like the door to the apartment block, it buckled and flew open. Eva didn't fire. There was no target. Well, not a live one.

An old woman in a tattered house dress stared at Eva, her eyes wide with shock. Her body slumped backwards in a recliner, and there was a clean bullet hole in the centre of her forehead. Eva touched the woman's neck. No pulse, but she was still warm. A fresh kill.

Isabella must have executed her to get to the balcony. This wasn't Isabella's apartment. She'd killed the old woman purely to get a shot at the drone.

Isabella was a cold-blooded murderer.

A quick search of the apartment failed to reveal her target. Isabella was somewhere else in the complex. There were five more apartments—too many to explore one by one. Eva needed to narrow down the search.

Returning to the landing, Eva tucked the pistol into the back of her jeans and casually pulled the fire alarm. In seconds a shrill siren sounded. Tenants piled out, wearing undershirts and carrying children. Within a minute, all the apartments had been evacuated. Except one.

Eva flicked off the alarm.

Extracting her gun, she trod towards apartment four. This time Eva was certain Isabella would be inside waiting for her. That meant caution was the advisable course of action. It was obvious she would stop at nothing to protect herself.

Eva shot the lock off the door and took cover beside it, her back against a solid brick wall. The door squeaked as it slowly swung open. The silence from inside the apartment was deafening.

After a nervous exhale, Eva pushed herself off the wall and grasped her pistol with both hands. Her prey knew she was coming, was armed, and was far more experienced than Eva.

Yeah, but does she know all the lyrics to REM's "It's the End of the World as We Know It"?

Eva stepped into the small hallway, gun ready. It was as quiet as a politician's conscience. The room wasn't as well appointed as the other apartment she'd seen, with only stark furnishings: bare wooden floorboards, a couch, a small table and chairs and a TV.

Suddenly a small black metallic device about the size of a hockey puck slid across the floor. Eva clenched her eyes shut, opened her mouth and covered her ears.

The flash grenade exploded in a burst of light and noise. A split second later Isabella dove out of the bedroom, gun aimed at Eva.

Too slow.

Eva was ready for her. The second Isabella emerged, Eva fired. The bullet hit the revolver in Isabella's hand, smacking it from her grasp. Isabella hit the floor hard. Eva fired twice more, close to Isabella's writhing body, to ensure she had her full and undivided attention.

Isabella, unarmed and clutching what had until recently been her firing hand, glared up at Eva, pure hatred oozing from every pore.

"'ow did you recover from the flash grenade so soon?"

Eva grinned as she stepped towards her. "Years in the front row of Aussie rock gigs, bitch."

It wasn't entirely true. Eva had been trained on how to handle flash grenades, but she'd also been to plenty of ear-bleeding rock concerts in her time. Eva didn't know if she shouted her answer due to the ringing in her ears. It didn't matter. She had Isabella exactly where she wanted her. A cursory search revealed no other weapons on Isabella's body.

Eva grabbed a fistful of Isabella's hair and dragged her across the floor to a kitchen chair. Using various kitchen electrical cords, she tied Isabella to the chair.

"I think it's time you and I had a little chat."

CHAPTER NINE

It took a while —and plenty of jaw exercises—for Eva's hearing to return. When it finally came good, Eva was ready to begin her interrogation.

Isabella appeared genuinely shaken that she'd been taken down by a rookie agent.

Too bad, Spunktrumpet.

"'ow did you find me?"

"Your own words Isabella, several times over. Do you remember our first meeting?"

Eva tugged at a restraint, tightening it, to emphasise the point. Isabella grunted.

"I do remember, yes."

Eva nodded and paced around her captive. "You made some joke about a meme, but after that you said something telling. You said that lies work best when they contain an element of truth. Do you remember?"

Isabella glared at her.

"So, when you later told me about the café near your home growing up, I found out where you truly grew up and worked back from there. It seems your safest place in the world betrayed you." She let that hang in the air for a moment. "Speaking of betrayal." She slapped Isabella hard across the face. "That was for Volmer."

Isabella sneered. "That little man was about to give you every-thing. Worse, 'e would have spilled all to the BVT."

"What was he going to spill, Isabella?"

The DGSE agent tilted her head, a red blemish materialising on the right side of her face. She tutted, then rolled her eyes, as if to say, *not that easy.*

"Then what can you tell me?" Eva folded her arms and assessed Isabella. "Straight or lesbian?"

Isabella pursed her lips and lifted an eyebrow at the question. "I hate to disappoint you, but I am straight."

"What was with all the lesbian talk?"

She shrugged. "All part of the game."

"And if I took you up on the offer in the hotel room?"

Isabella took a moment to think about it. "Then we would have learned many things together I think, yes?"

Eva recommenced her pacing, formulating another tack to try. Isabella was well-versed in interrogation. This was going to be tough.

Isabella's arms pulled against the restraints. "I do not under-stand why you 'ave tied me up like this, Eva. In spite of all the events, I thought we were friends. I could 'ave killed you back in Vienna, at the 'otel, but I did not."

"You ran me over."

Isabella frowned. "In my defence, you were shooting at me."

"You hit me with goddamn a car!"

"But I did not kill you, no? I did not reverse over you, I did not fire my weapon at you. That is quite magnanimous of me, yes? You see? Friends."

Eva wasn't getting anywhere. She decided to change the subject.

"The identities of the suicide bombers. The DGSE knew them almost instantly. How?"

Isabella poked out her chin. "The DGSE, we are incredibly good at what we do."

"Nobody is that good. Someone knew beforehand, and I think it was you." Eva planted her fists on her hips. "I initially assumed they'd been identified quickly because Mustafa and the others had known terrorist links. But they didn't. None of those kids had links with any terrorist organisation. The funny thing is, that's not what you told me. So my question is, how did the DGSE know their identities?"

Isabella shrugged, as innocent as a sleazy guy asking if you wanted a teabag.

Eva went on. "You knew the attack was coming, Isabella. Either you alone or people within the DGSE, but you knew those bombers were going to strike. You knew innocent people were going to die, and I want to know why."

The chatty Isabella was suddenly quite cagey. She pursed her lips and shook her head as if to say, *preposterous*. Eva didn't believe it. Isabella was involved, and Eva wanted to know how—and, more importantly, why.

Eva pulled up a flimsy wooden chair in front of Isabella. Straddling it, she stared into Isabella's eyes. "What about the families of your victims, Isabella? A hundred and ten people died with your bombs. Don't you feel guilty about that?"

The woman's face was as stone cold as a glacier. Eva would keep poking until she found a kink in the armour.

"What about the families of those children you so blatantly exploited? Hmmm? How would they feel about you sacrificing their sons for your own sick ends?"

The disdain on Isabella's face morphed. It was no longer tinged with contempt. It was something else entirely. It was menacing, vicious.

"They are classe inférieure," Isabella spat. "These people are all the same, whether they call themselves terrorists or not. They feed off my country like dogs, sucking us dry until we 'ave nothing left. 'ow do I feel about 'urting families like this? I feel nothing for them."

Eva tilted closer. "Careful there, Isabella, your prejudice is showing. Not exactly liberty, equality and fraternity, now is it?" Eva leaned back. "The families are innocent. They did nothing wrong until you stuck your hooks in their children, but they'll be tarred as terrorist sympathisers, or worse, for the rest of their lives. You murdered their sons, their babies, for what? Don't you care about that at all?"

The way Isabella's face transformed back into casual detachment made it plain she didn't. She seemed not to care about the wreckage she'd wrought, on both the terrorist victims and the families of the perpetrators. She truly was heartless.

Eva had gotten a reaction by mentioning the suicide bombers. She decided to push it further.

"Again, I come back to your motive, Isabella. Forcing these kids to commit acts of terror isn't going to rid your country of anyone of colour or of a certain religion. Your president spent time yesterday at a mosque, mending relations. So why sanction an act of terrorism? To what end?"

Isabella gave a mirthless leer. "You think this is about terrorism?"

Eva pushed herself away from the chair. It was virtually the same phrase Justin had uttered on top of the Ferris wheel. If it wasn't about terrorism, what the hell was it about?

For all the talk, Eva felt that she wasn't getting anywhere. She needed concrete resolutions, not a vague collection of semi-answers. This was going to take a while.

Just as she was about to launch into another round of questions, there was a deafening bang on the front door. Eva pulled out her pistol and aimed it at Isabella. She placed an index finger to her lips. *Quiet.*

To emphasise the point, she wrapped a tea towel around Isabella's mouth, forming an impromptu gag. She pointed at her to stay put. Isabella rolled her eyes. She wasn't exactly going anywhere.

In French, Eva called out, "Who is it?"

A loud muffled male voice replied, "Fire brigade, ma'am. We

are checking each of the apartments after the alarm. May I come in?"

Eva peered through the peephole, gun barrel pointed at the door. On the other side was a member of the fire brigade, complete with full face respirator. That would explain the muffled voice.

"All good here, thank you!"

"Ma'am, I need to check, if that is alright? Regulations."

Behind the firefighter, other similarly clad members of the fire brigade were talking to various residents. They were all doing so with wide open doors.

"Just a second, I'll put some clothes on," Eva said, rushing back to Isabella.

She tilted the chair and dragged Isabella to the bathroom. Isabella's gagged protests were silenced when Eva shut the door.

Eva rushed to the door and opened it. The large bulky man nodded and gave a tweak of his helmet.

"Thank you, ma'am. Now if I could have a quick scout of the apartment to ensure everything is alright."

Eva swivelled her shoulders seductively. "Are you sure that's necessary?" She wasn't happy about resorting to flirtation. It rubbed against her feminist tendencies. "I'm pretty sure there's no fire."

She thought about adding, 'unless you count in my pants', but thought it would be a bit much.

"I'll only be a minute," he said as he stepped into the apartment.

"The kitchen is over there," Eva said in the most girlish voice she could muster.

Stay out of the bathroom! Eva tried to project the thought into the man's head.

He roamed about the apartment, giving the oven a superficial inspection. He was certainly a big bastard. Six-four and could have played in the backline of a rugby team.

Thankfully he didn't head for the bathroom, but he didn't seem to moving towards the front door either. There was something about his manner that put Eva on edge. Why the respirator when his fellow firefighters didn't have theirs on? Why hadn't he even glanced at the smoke detectors? Eva could see two from where she was standing.

"Excuse me," Eva said, walking towards him, "what exactly is it that you're—"

The backhand sent her flying. Eva's back slammed into the kitchen table and her nose exploded in a fireball of pain. For man of his bulk he moved like lightning. He slammed the front door closed and bounded towards her.

Eva extracted the gun from behind her back, but before she could even manage to bring it around, the big man barrelled his shoulder into her. The blow sent her flying backwards. The gun flew from her hand and landed somewhere near the couch, while Eva smacked into the fridge, hard. The world spun in and out of focus. No matter what, she had to stay on her feet.

Eva wiped the blood cascading from her nose. *Time for some Krav Maga, you fuckmuppet.*

Eva crouched into her fighting stance and cracked her neck. "Let's do this, Marshmallow."

The big man took a swing, a big haymaker. Eva ducked and let his overbalance propel him forward. She used her mass to push him off balance, sending him crashing into the fridge.

That's one. Eva still owed him for the first cheap shot.

"Who the hell are you?" she demanded.

The man didn't answer, he simply rasped through the respirator. His next punch wasn't as wild as the last. Eva managed to duck the blow and get in a few rib shots, but not enough to harm a unit of his size. She was outmatched. She needed to get out of the apartment, but there was no way she was leaving Isabella behind.

Before Eva could get in position, the man was at her again. Two massive fists flying, he went for successive headshots. Eva weaved past the first, but caught the better part of the second, which sent her careening across the carpet.

A small chuckle escaped the brute's mask. It stopped quickly when he realised what Eva was up to. She'd used the force of the blow to fling herself across the room. Right near where her gun was.

As Eva scrambled for her gun she heard the shot. The pain struck her at the same instant. The bastard had shot her in the lower back. It was excruciating. She screamed and clutched at the wound. Blood flooded through her fingers, and her vision lurched into blackness.

She was going to pass out from the pain.

The brute kicked away Eva's gun, forever out of her grasp, then strode into the bathroom. Moments later, as Eva clung to the last of her consciousness, Isabella emerged, a triumphant sneer spread across her evil features.

She knelt down, her face level with Eva's, and tilted her head curiously, but didn't say anything. She observed the blood spurting out of Eva's wound and grinned.

She traced a finger across Eva's arm, then slid it down her back. She carefully lifted Eva's weak hands, which had been clenching her wound. Isabella examined the lesion and gave a *tsk tsk*. She then extended a finger and plunged it directly into the bullet hole.

Eva shrieked in mind-numbing pain.

Isabella covered Eva's mouth and said soothingly, "Shhh, my love, shhh." She yelled in Eva's ear so she could be heard over the screaming. "Do you remember the last time we spoke in Vienna?"

Eva couldn't focus on anything. The pain was beyond comprehension. She writhed on the floor, slipping in the pool of her own blood.

Isabella went on. "I do. I told you I would always 'ave your back." She sunk her finger further into the bullet wound and Eva screamed like never before.

She blacked out.

CHAPTER TEN

Eva was jolted awake by a splash of water in her face. She spluttered and strained against the ties that bound her to the same flimsy wooden chair she'd tied Isabella to. The tide had turned, but now she knew how vicious Isabella could be.

Friend, hey? She glared at her captor.

"Oh, do not look at me like that," Isabella said with a pout. "It could 'ave been much worse. I could 'ave thrown coffee in your face, no?"

If there's coffee to be thrown, that's my job, Eva thought. She knew how to make that shit burn.

Eva assessed her situation. The dull ache in her back meant she'd been dosed up on something to deal with the pain. She rubbed her back against the chair. Something under her t-shirt crinkled, but she couldn't quite feel it. The wound was numb.

They needed Eva alive for some reason. She could only speculate as to why. Perhaps Isabella needed answers. Was Eva working with a team? Did the DGSE or MI6 know where she was?

They were good questions. It was a pity the answers were no. Eva was on her own. Nobody knew where she was. There was no backup. No one would come for her. The SAS wouldn't be swinging in on ropes and telling everyone how awesome they were. No one would save her.

Eva could hear the shower running. She guessed it was the fake fireman. At least, she assumed he was fake. Eva didn't know much about the Paris fire brigade, but she suspected beating up women wasn't usually part of the service.

Given the circumstances, Eva had to assume Isabella had gone rogue. She was hiding out, had been disguised, she'd murdered an innocent French citizen and had tended to Eva's wounds personally rather than taking her to a hospital. Plus, there was no one else in the room. No witnesses.

Isabella leaned against the kitchen table. She'd changed her outfit. This one matched her curves instead of disguising them. Two pistols lay beside her on the table, as well as an assortment of armaments. Based on the equipment, Isabella had come prepared for a siege. The weapons were all too far away for Eva's liking.

"Thirteen dollars." Eva's voice was hoarse and barely audible.

Isabella leaned in. "What was that?"

"Thirteen. Dollars." Eva struggled to speak. She was weak. Very weak.

Isabella shook her head, not comprehending.

"When we first met," Eva said, fighting for each word, "I said if I had a dollar for every time I'd been tied up, I'd have twelve dollars. It's up to thirteen now."

Genuine amusement spread across Isabella's features. She shook her head. "You amaze me every time we meet, Eva Destruction. Just when I think I 'ave you figured out, you come up with something new."

Eva did her best to sound strong. "You owe me a dollar."

Isabella stroked one of the pistols. "Perhaps I do, but," she tilted her head, "do you really think you're going to live long enough to spend it?"

Doing her best to clear her head, Eva glared at Isabella. "The DGSE must be so proud of the little monster they've created."

Isabella shook her head. "You are not cut out for espionage. You are too weak, too feeble. You still have morals, for goodness sake. This profession is not for you. Only bastards are suited to this life, yes? You 'ave to be 'eartless to be a spy, Eva."

Heartless? Eva wasn't heartless. She was many things: a decent dancer, a seasoned drinker, a bar room brawler. But heartless? No. Yet another person doubting her suitability for the job. Not that it mattered. Unless she escaped, she'd be nothing but landfill and a name on the MI6 memorial wall.

The water in the bathroom was turned off, followed by the sound of a shower curtain being pulled back. After a few moments, the man who'd beaten the crap out of Eva marched into the living area with a towel wrapped around his waist. The flecks of grey didn't mask the fact that he was in exceptionally good physical shape for a man in his fifties.

He strode over to Isabella and gave her a deep, passionate kiss. Once he extracted himself from Isabella's embrace, he gave Eva a wink and went to the fridge to grab a beer.

There was no need for introductions. Eva knew who he was. Eva knew everything about him.

Born in Essex, he'd joined the British Army at sixteen. He'd soon qualified as a Para, Parachute Regiment, and worked his way through the ranks. From there he'd quit the armed forces and joined MI6 as a field agent. Over the next two decades he'd excelled in many international missions, earning praise and distinctions. He'd racked up quite the list of achievements.

He was also meant to be dead.

Alexander Bourke was the man Eva had been tasked with finding on her original mission. It seemed obvious now why a supposedly dead MI6 agent had been seen near Lyon; he'd been working with Isabella.

If she had a free leg she would have kicked herself. Alex was Alexis. Of course he was. Eva had presumed Isabella's fellow agent would have been from the DGSE, not MI6.

The not-dead Alex slithered up to Isabella and wrapped his muscular arm around her. They stared at Eva, as if admiring a treasured pet. Isabella nestled into his bare chest. Eva wasn't sure her nausea was entirely related to her injury.

Fighting through the haze of drugs and pain, Eva said, "You look better with the mask on."

Alex didn't take his eyes off Eva. He said, "You're right, she is sassy. Quite the attitude." He frowned approvingly. "Tough, too."

"Now now, my love, don't be getting ideas." She patted his brawny thigh. "She'll rip your throat out given 'alf a chance. This one's not a plaything."

Alex looked Eva up and down. "Shame."

There was a familiarity and warmth in their banter. They seemed to actually be in love. Sick and twisted love, but love nonetheless. Psychopaths in love sounded like a movie from the 90s.

Eva regarded Isabella. "Lies work best when they contain an element of truth." She jutted her chin at Alex. "This is 'Alexis'. The person you said you loved more than life itself."

Isabella and Alex grinned at one another, but said nothing.

Eva went on. "The mission you told me about, the one where you were impulsive and Alexis died, that was another lie, wasn't it? He didn't die, he just appeared to, as far as MI6 were concerned. Then he went off and set up The Tempest. Am I right?"

Isabella didn't reply, just stroked Alex's chest.

After a swig of beer, Alex said, "She's smart, too."

All the pieces were starting to fall into place—all except the keystone. The one piece that made everything fit together.

"Why?"

Neither replied. Alex took a big gulp of beer, draining the bottle. He turned to Eva. "You could at least offer your appreciation."

She shook her head. "For what?"

He nodded at Eva's midriff. "The bullet missed all your major organs".

"Am I meant to thank you for shooting me in the back? Did you get thank you notes from all your terrorist victims? Gee, thanks for blowing off my body parts and burning me alive, you're the best. Love and kisses."

"Okay, perhaps appreciation was too much, but you could at least admire the craftsmanship."

"The what?"

He sighed. "See, if I'd hit a lung or your heart, you'd be dead in no time. With that injury you could last days, weeks if we tend to it well enough. Imagine the information we could extract in that time. All the fun we could have while you bleed out. What a time we'll have."

There it was. The veiled threat. Not even that veiled. Eva wouldn't be getting out of this alive. They'd healed her just enough to extract the information they needed, then she was done for. There would be torture. There would be pain. There would be death.

"So, my love, the question of the 'our is, who knows you are 'ere?" Isabella asked. "As we 'aven't 'ad anyone kick in the doors yet, I'm assuming not many?"

Eva squared her jaw. "Everyone."

"Everyone?" Isabella replied mockingly.

"Yep," Eva said confidently. "MI6, the DGSE, MI5, SAS, CIA, Mossad, Green Berets, Delta Force, the Mormon Tabernacle Choir, David Hasselhoff, Fozzie the Bear, fucken' everyone."

Isabella and Alex laughed. Eva didn't like those laughs. Sure, she thought she was naturally pretty funny, but she didn't think it was her banter that amused them, More like her desperation.

It was obvious Eva didn't have any backup. She would die in this shitty apartment. If she was going to perish, she at least wanted to die with some answers.

"What I don't get," she began, "is why you would want to recruit young kids to blow themselves up? There's plenty who will do it for free without your help."

Alex opened the fridge and pulled out another beer. "True, but not when we need them to."

Isabella poked him in the ribs, as if to silence him.

Alex shrugged and took another drink. "Who's she going to tell?"

The DGSE agent rolled her eyes and tilted her head, as if to say, *go ahead*. Alex grinned.

Over three beers, Alex answered Eva's question in great detail.

Their joint mission had been to track a Belgian scientist who was selling black market materials. They'd tracked him to a warehouse in Sarajevo where he was trading plutonium for bars of gold.

Like Isabella had told Eva back in Vienna, the mission went south. Isabella rushed in recklessly, the scientist died in the crossfire and Alex was badly wounded.

Even before the mission, he and Isabella had become jaded with espionage. While he slowly bled out and they awaited extraction, they formed a plan. Alex would fake his own death, leave MI6 behind and use his skills to create a new enterprise. They set the warehouse on fire, dressing one of the terrorists as Alex, and had Isabella tell the story of how Alex had sacrificed himself for her. Standing orders were that only live agents would be extracted, so MI6 thought Alex was a pile of ash in Sarajevo.

"But I still don't get it," Eva said. "To what end? A spy for hire is nothing new. I'm sure freelance ex-agents are a common thing."

Isabella and Alex beamed at one another. He shook his head. "This isn't about spying on a politician's wife or being a gun for hire for a drug cartel. It's much grander than that. No one has ever tried this before." He waited, enjoying the dramatic pause. "We call ourselves The Tempest. We've been using acts of terrorism to manipulate the stock market."

If he was expecting a round of applause, he was plumb out of luck.

There it was The Tempest was Alex and Isabella. They were the shadow organisation behind it all. This wasn't revolution, this was profit.

Alex went on. "If you'll excuse me for using the phrase, we've been making a killing."

If the evilness of their scheme wasn't enough, their smugness was sufficient justification to execute them in the slowest manner possible. What sort of sadistic bastard killed innocent people for fun and profit?

Isabella rolled her eyes. "Oh, don't judge me with those self-righteous eyes. You don't think your government does the same every other week? What do you think wars are about, my love? Being right? No, they're about profit. Just like this."

They were truly insane. *Terrorism for profit.* There was no insult vile enough for these two.

Alex oozed smugness. "Time an attack here, bump up a stock there. It's pure genius. I can't believe no one has tried it before."

"Maybe nobody has been as sadistic and twisted as you two fucking crazy bellend slapping spunktrumpets."

"Oh, they 'ave been, darling," Isabella said, "believe me. They just 'aven't 'ad our vision."

"So, what? You pick innocent kids off the street, tell them they're terrorists and strap bombs to them? Jesus Christ."

"That was Nur's job." Isabella nodded at Eva. "You call him Justin Bieber. 'e was good at convincing them they were on their way to paradise. He could talk the talk, that is for sure. It is a shame we 'ave to find a replacement for 'im."

"Maybe you shouldn't have killed him then?" Eva glared.

"Well, I couldn't risk 'im spilling everything, now could I?"

It was clear Eva was dealing with two psychopaths. Cold-blooded, unfeelingly merciless and without pity. They were truly vile. If she had half a chance Eva would slash their throats for the world to be rid of them.

"I see you're impressed," Alex said, his words dripping with sarcasm. "It was all Isabella's idea. Brilliance personified, when you think about it. Invest in oil stocks and blow up a tanker in the Persian Gulf. Need prices to go down? Let an Arab country foil a terrorist plot. Simple economics."

"What was Lyon? I assume something to do with the NATO summit?"

"Oh yes," Isabella smiled. "Defence stocks went through the roof. They were going to announce a scale back on spending. We bought up big at a ridiculously low price and ta da, made quite a sizable profit with minimal effort."

"But all those blameless people died. Those suicide bomber kids died. For what? A few pieces of silver?"

"Far more than that!" Alex boomed. His face was angry. "I've seen my compatriots, my friends, die because of politics. Government officials don't care about espionage or what is right or wrong —they care about the next election and the state of the economy. When they had to choose between a two per cent swing in some election or letting one of my friends die alone, bleeding out in the snow in the middle of Siberia, guess which one they chose? We are mere commodities. I simply took their game to the next level. Everyone is dispensable in the new world economy. The funds we're raising will support people like us, and their families. They'll live like the leaders who don't give two shits about their lot. They'll be compensated like they should have been years ago, not sacrificed on the altar of an election platform."

"It's blood money," Eva spat. "It will be tainted with the lives of those innocent people you cut down."

Alex shook his head condescendingly, as if talking to an ignorant child. "All money is tainted, girl. You think that steak you ate last week was from a humanely treated animal? You think that cheap phone you own wasn't manufactured by economic slave children who don't die early, tortured deaths? Wake up. We're reaping vengeance on those who believe life is cheap, by using their own tactics against them."

They were truly insane. Eva didn't buy the added moralising; it was pure justification for their blatant greed. Reason wouldn't get through to them. She doubted anything would.

"Why are you telling me all this?" Eva dreaded the answer.

Alex gave an embarrassed shrug. "It's a bit 80s bad guy confession, isn't it? But it doesn't really matter. You know you'll die here, right? Telling you all this just cements that in your mind. Now that you know we can't let you live, you'll provide us with answers more quickly."

"Oh, gee, you're right. Can you pass me that pencil over there?" Eva nodded to one by the coffee table.

Alex picked it up and walked towards her, a curious expression on his face. He twirled it in his fingers like a wannabe-drummer. "Why on earth would you need a pencil?"

"I need to write my last will and testament, obviously. I'm

going to leave Isabella my spoon collection. Would you be interested in my assortment of My Little Pony hair ties?"

Alex placed the pencil on the table and towered over her. "Sarcasm won't save you, bitch. MI6 won't save you. Nothing will. You think you're smart now, but you'll be spilling your guts soon enough, begging us to end the pain."

"What pain?" Eva asked.

Why did you ask that, Twatmonkey?

Isabella leapt from the table, twisted Eva's body and without preamble punched her wound. Pain enveloped Eva completely. The agony was complete. Her vision was engulfed by intense, excruciating light.

"Who knows you are 'ere?" Isabella screamed, followed by another punch. "Who did you tell?"

Eva had never experienced anything so intense. The agony overwhelmed her. The questions and blows kept coming; Isabella never let up. She took delight in seeing Eva suffer. She panted like she was getting off on it. The woman was sick.

The beating and questions were relentless.

Eva passed out.

When Eva came to, Isabella and Alex were nestled in each other's arms on the couch. It was a comfortable embrace, like two lovers watching television. Except there was no television. They seemed to be scrutinising a smartphone, no doubt reading news of their exploits. The two spies faced away from Eva, towards the door. Alex's gun lay next to them on the armrest, alongside Eva's. Eva kept her eyes mostly closed, so they'd think she was still out if they turned around.

"What about a car accident?" Isabella asked.

Alex gave a disapproving grunt. "I'm still inclined to get rid of her in another terrorist act."

"No, my love," Isabella said in a soothing voice. "Even if we still had Nur and his little contacts, what would be the point? If we could use one of the fresh patsies, why would we waste someone we 'ad spent all that time and money readying for 'er?" Isabella nodded in Eva's general direction. "It takes so long to groom them, we do not want to sacrifice one for no financial gain, no?"

There was the sound of a kiss. Alex said, "You are a practical capitalist, my dear."

Isabella snapped her fingers. "'ow about we strip 'er naked. Snap 'er neck and throw 'er off a bridge? They will not know if it is suicide, assault or what."

"Perfect!" Alex replied, as if they'd just chosen what takeaway to order.

Eva's fate was sealed. All she needed to do now was be tortured more, suffer and die.

Except that wasn't going to happen. Eva Destruction was not one to lie down and simply hope for the best. She was a survivor. She was a fighter. And not a clean one, either. She may have been weak from torture, but Eva still had a pulse. That was enough.

On the kitchen table were two spare clips of ammunition. Useless without a gun. But next to them, there was something she could use. A desperate plan formed in her mind. It was haphazard at best, laughable at worst, but it would do.

Eva readied herself as best she could without arousing attention. Muscles tensed. She drew air into her lungs, knowing they would soon be put to the test. There would be no second chances, no do-overs. Mess this up and she was dead.

Don't fuck it up, Dildo Breath.

Eva used her feet to propel herself skyward. She kicked out her shackled legs so the rear of the flimsy chair hit the ground hard.

It landed with a crash, and the rickety furniture splintered under her weight. Every part of Eva was pummelled with agony. Her captors' heads snapped around. Eva rolled around to fragment the chair further, then got to her feet. Her legs and arms were still bound, but she could move.

As fast as her aching limbs would let her, Eva reached for the device on the table and hurled it at Isabella and Alex. It sailed between them, hitting neither.

Alex untangled himself from his lover's arms and scrambled for a gun. Eva jabbed her right arm at Alex. The chair leg slid from the ties and projected directly at his head. He ducked out of the way, the wooden projectile missing him by centimetres. A wry smile crossed his lips as he aimed the gun at Eva, as if to say, *you missed your chance, bitch.*

The flash grenade exploded behind them. Eva picked up the other chair and hurled it at the kitchen window. The glass fractured as the chair sailed through it. Eva stepped onto the table, ready to leap through.

But Alex had other ideas.

The big man clomped across the floor, his eyes unfocused, stunned by the grenade. His lumbering hand grabbed Eva's wrist. She snatched the only thing available to her.

A pencil.

She plunged the sharp object into Alex's bulging neck. It sank into his flesh and instantly a geyser of blood spurted from his carotid artery. He screamed in pain. Eva used her palm to ram in the pencil further into his neck. He wheeled backwards, groping at the haemorrhage.

Not waiting another second, Eva propelled herself at the window. She leapt through the fractured gap, not knowing what was on the other side.

Eva plunged from the window, clutching at the air. The fall from the second floor wasn't as high as she'd thought. The atrium over the apartment foyer hurtled towards her. Eva collided with it awkwardly, and a fraction of a second later it shattered from the impact. Eva crashed through and landed heavily on the floor, a barrage of glass fragments showering around her.

She was bruised, cut and winded. But alive. The atrium had broken her fall. There was no time to be thankful. Eva pushed herself up with weakened arms and forced her exhausted body to keep moving.

The pain was unbearable. Her body screamed for her to stop, to rest. But if she did, she'd be dead. With a wheezing chest, Eva lurched forward.

She ripped part of her t-shirt and wrapped it around an elongated shard of glass. With a cough and a splutter, she staggered towards the front entrance. As she yanked it open, bullets shattered the glass above her head. They were firing blindly at her, but it was too late. She was through the door.

Lurching onto the street, Eva wobbled on unsteady legs. Passers-by gasped at her bloodied and bruised appearance. Or it may have been the giant shard of glass she wielded.

Isabella and Alex would be on their way down by now. She had to move. An old white beat-up Citroën with a pizza sign on its roof sped down the narrow street. Eva staggered onto the road and held the shard out menacingly. The driver skidded to a halt.

Through the open front window, Eva stabbed the air in front of the driver's terrified face. He slid across to the passenger side, away from the crazy lady with the glass.

In heavily accented French, he asked, "Is this a carjacking?"

Eva threw the car in gear and took off. "No, just an exceptionally aggressive alternate delivery."

As the aged car sped around the corner, Eva glanced at the rear-view mirror and saw Alex and Isabella burst from the apartment block. They scanned the street for any sign of Eva, but she was already gone. Alex clutched his bleeding neck.

It seemed MI6's focus on stabbing people with pencils had finally paid off. At least Eva had utilised one thing she'd learned. She hoped lead poisoning was fatal.

For several blocks, Eva remained mute, using every ounce of energy she had left to keep the car on the road. Her eyelids were leaden, every fibre of her body screamed for her to shut down. She couldn't let that happen.

Suddenly everything turned black. Eva was jolted awake by the screech of car horns and the high-pitched squealing of the delivery driver. She'd veered into oncoming traffic. She fought the wheel to regain control of the vehicle.

At the first chance she got, Eva pulled the car over and turned to the driver. "Sorry about that. Maybe you could drive." She saw the terror in his eyes. "I'm not here to hurt you."

"Your very big piece of glass says otherwise."

"Sorry." She put the glass down. "I was escaping some bad people. You saved my life. Thanks."

"Okay." His clear eyes were sceptical.

"My organisation will give you a reward," Eva said apologetically. "I'm sorry if I scared you back there."

The driver's shoulders relaxed. He nodded. They swapped seats and the driver took off for the hospital. As they drove in silence, Eva flipped open one of the pizza boxes in the back seat.

"Is that Hawaiian? Sweet." She took a bite. It was the single most delicious thing Eva had ever tasted.

"Please do not eat my pizzas," the driver said with a frown.

Eva took another bite. She felt revitalised. "Can I borrow your phone?"

The driver gave her a sideways glance. "Do I have a choice?"

"You always have a choice, dude."

The driver shrugged and extracted a phone from his pocket. "Who are you calling?"

"The big guns."

CHAPTER ELEVEN

Eva felt like a petulant child waiting to see the principal. She sat in the hospital chair, watching the rain cascade down the window. After being patched up she felt a million Australian dollars. Given the current exchange rate, that was pretty good.

She'd called Paul from the pizza delivery car. Her boss/mate had been livid and relieved at the same time. That's who she was waiting for in the hospital room. He'd jumped on the first available flight to Paris and was on his way up in the elevator. Eva wasn't entirely sure what her fate would be. A promotion was definitely out; a treason charge was more likely.

When she'd been admitted to hospital, she'd told her story to the doctors and they'd immediately called the police. Within minutes cops swarmed around her. She wasn't one hundred per cent sure if they were protecting her or guarding her.

The doctors said she'd live, but that the bullet wound was likely infected, and that the trauma to the lesion would likely leave a nasty scar. Bikinis would be out. It was a small price to pay.

Mohamed the delivery driver would be given a citation and a hefty reward by His Majesty's government. Eva had even called his boss to apologise for the late delivery, and the missing pizza slices.

The sound of a knock made Eva turn. Paul's beaming face poked around the door.

"I hear this is the incredibly-daft-but-lucky-Aussie wing."

Eva leapt out of her chair and instantly regretted it. The painkillers were wearing off, and every part of her hurt. She was dizzy, but still managed to meet the tall, lanky Englishman halfway.

He wrapped his big arms around her but didn't squeeze as tightly as he normally did. At least he remembered she had severe injuries, even if she'd forgotten. Right now he wasn't her boss, he was her friend. Albeit a slightly pissed one.

They sat and chatted for a while. Eva could tell he was doing his best to remain calm, mainly due to what she'd been through. She knew him well enough to know he was also furious. She'd disobeyed a direct order. *His* direct order. She'd put herself in harm's way. Others had died, and the perpetrators had gotten away, yet again.

"What happens next?" Eva asked.

"Well, I was thinking I'd try and find a decent pub in this godforsaken country. Do you think they even do pints here?"

"Paul, I mean with me, and with Isabella and Alex."

"Well now, you're a prickly one."

"Give a girl a break. I haven't been able to shave my legs in days."

"Funny," Paul said, showing no sign of amusement. "I've done some spin with the top brass. Took some doing, let me tell you. They think you were never off the case, and that I only said you were to put off anyone in contact with Alex or the DGSE."

"Good spin," Eva said, genuinely impressed.

"Any more and I'd be a bloody whirling dervish," Paul said, rubbing the back of his neck. "You know you're getting me an awesome birthday present this year, right? None of that nice socks rubbish. A big-arse Lego set, like a Millennium Falcon or something. Nancy will hate it, but I think it's the least you can do."

"Two birthdays," Eva said firmly.

"Bloody right." Paul grinned.

Eva knew he didn't actually expect her to buy him the gift, which was all the more reason she would. "And Isabella?"

A frown. "I'd like to say even the DGSE can't ignore this one, but they're trying bloody hard to. An agent cavorting with a supposedly dead foreign agent and bombing her own country is pretty damning stuff. If she worked for MI6 she definitely wouldn't be invited to the office Christmas party, but the Frenchies are being so damned cagey. They're denying her involvement, of course. An all-points bulletin, or whatever their damn equivalent is, has been issued for an identikit likeness of Alex."

"Not Isabella?" Eva asked with a scowl.

Paul gave a shake of his head. "I have a nasty feeling they're going to sweep this one under the carpet. My hope is that the two of them flee France and we catch them on foreign soil, because I doubt Isabella will see the inside of a courtroom."

Before Eva could raise a protest, Paul lifted his palm. "And for pretty much the same reason, we need to find Alex before the Frenchies do. Can you imagine the ruckus that will ensue if a former MI6 agent is connected to terrorist attacks in France? We'd be thrown out of 9 Eyes, NATO, the G8, UAFA, and the Tin Tin official fan club."

"Pretty sure Tin Tin is Belgian."

"Whatever," Paul said, then his face turned grave once more. "We need to find the buggers first. The French authorities have dropped a net on the city, but the place is a rat's nest. You could hide out for years and never be detected." He poked his chin at Eva. "Good work on finding her, by the way. We'll make an agent out of you yet."

"So I'm not fired?" Eva asked.

It amazed her how much she cared about the answer.

Paul dropped one of his famous long pauses. "If you're not you came bloody close to the wire, Missy. We'll have to see. The smart money would be on you being turfed out on your skinny white arse, but you know me, I'm not that smart."

There was still hope. Even if she got away with being in France when she shouldn't have been, there'd been too many failures in her mission. Too many missed chances. Too many lost lives. MI6 would have a hard time justifying the mouthy, inexperienced Australian keeping her job.

Eva didn't answer, but surveyed the scene outside her window. After a pause of her own, she said, "I want to be there. I want to see their faces when they're caught."

"Evie, you're getting on the next plane—"

"The bastard shot me. She stuck her damn finger in my hole. Not a good hole, either. A very bad hole, Paul. Very bad. I want to see them go down, and not on each other."

"We don't even know where they are, love. These are two highly trained and experienced spies. They know how to go underground. It's what they do. It could be weeks, if at all. It could—"

Paul's phone rang. They smirked at one another.

"If this was a movie," Eva nodded at his phone, "now would be the time for someone to say they've been cornered."

Paul answered the call and listened. After uttering "Uh-huh" a few times, he rang off.

"Well," he said. "I guess life can be like a movie sometimes."

As much as Eva hated to admit it, technology had succeeded yet again. To the chagrin of privacy advocates, since the attacks the French government had hooked its claws into private CCTV networks in the name of homeland security. The upshot was that they had tens of thousands of servers at their disposal, running facial recognition programs. It was a gross violation of privacy. It had also worked.

A person answering to Alex's description had been spotted at a train station. The photo was crystal clear: Alex and Isabella entering the main concourse of the Gare du Nord. There were also fuzzier photographs of them purchasing an international train pass and eating ice cream and laughing like tourists in love. Murder must be quite the aphrodisiac.

Alerts had immediately been triggered in every French government organisation with a passing interest in the attacks in Lyon. Given the worldwide profile of the crimes committed, every man and his dog wanted in on the arrest. Based on the phalanx of uniforms, Eva wouldn't have been surprised if the local dog catchers had been called in, too.

Gare du Nord was an international train station; the EuroStar to London left from there. The nearby Gare de I'Est train station was also being covered, as it had international destinations as well.

Eva assumed that even if they flew within the EU, airport scrutiny would be too tight. Rail travel could be more lax, so that's where they took their chance.

She and Paul stood on rue La Fayette, between the two stations, and watched the operation unfold. They were there in a purely ceremonial capacity, at the behest of the DGSE, perhaps as an olive branch, potentially to keep an eye on them. Their liaison had wandered off when the interdepartmental chest beating began.

Paul paced up and down the sidewalk. He was livid that he could do nothing while the French were about to capture Alex. In one move they would ruin MI6's reputation, and he was helpless to do anything about it. It should have been MI6's collar. They'd wanted him first. Paul didn't say it, but all this could have been avoided if Eva had caught him back in Lyon.

It hadn't been revealed that the photographs were of a former MI6 operative. As far as the agencies knew, he was merely a man with a description. When that information broke, the consequences would be catastrophic for MI6 and His Majesty's government. A former British spy involved in terrorist acts in France would be news everywhere. It would tarnish them forever.

If Paul had his way, he and Eva would grab Alex and take him back to the UK before the French authorities got their hooks into him, but that was unlikely. Paul's inability to do exactly that led him to pace even faster.

The station was surrounded by uniforms. There must have

been several hundred officers from various departments, all jock-eying for position and ownership of the shit-show.

There was an agreement that all forces would hold off and not close in until the order was given. A sensible plan. A logical one, even. Of course, it didn't work out that way.

The Prefect of Préfecture de police de Paris, or the head of the Paris police department, ordered his people to swarm the station, in direct contravention of the agreed strategy. All hell broke loose.

Representatives of various organisations tried to cover the same exit. While they argued with one another, passengers sailed right past. It was a textbook example of how not to run a dragnet. It would be laughable if their actions didn't mean the slaughtering bastards were going to slip through their fingers.

Across the road, Paul and Eva watched the shemozzle unfold. Clumps of commuters were streaming through while only the occasional one was challenged. There seemed to be no rhyme or reason to it. Even though she didn't smoke, Eva wanted to light one up and blow smoke in disgust.

Paul stared, open-mouthed, as a shoving match broke out between two uniformed groups. "It's like they're trying to re-enact the first days of the revolution. This is madness."

Being spotted at a train station had a sense of urgency to it, suggesting they had to leave right now. There was desperation to their tactic. It had also seemingly drawn every available French agent to the one location. Had they meant to be seen?

Through the phalanx of uniforms, four civilian figures emerged and headed toward the taxi ranks. Two figures in particular caught Eva's attention.

"There, in the red," Eva pointed toward a woman wearing a large black floppy hat and an ill-fitting red dress. "I know it's her. The way she moved, the way they hugged one another. It's them, I know it."

Paul squinted across the road and some distance away. The two had slipped behind a huddle of commuters waiting for taxis. He shook his head with a frown as if not seeing them. "The French are going mad trying to catch Alex, there's no way he wouldn't have been challenged. They're going to do everything they can. Despite what their national football team would have you believe, they're not idiots."

Eva eyed the chaos unfolding at the nearest exit. One officer took a swing at a rival department's officer, but was pulled back by his compatriots. Eva hefted an eyebrow at her boss.

Paul threw up his hand and yelled, "Taxi!"

A passing taxi skidded to a halt in front of them. As the taxi with woman in the black hat and her partner took off, Eva and Paul bundled into theirs.

To the driver, Eva said "I can't believe I'm going to say this, but," she sighed at the cliché, "follow that taxi".

The driver grinned at the challenge. Paul offered him an extra fifty Euros if he kept with them. The driver hunkered down behind the wheel like a rally driver, turned his peaked cap backwards and floored it. Eva wondered if he was related to the Viennese tram driver.

As they raced off, Eva said, "Fiver says they're still getting out of Paris on a train. They bought a rail pass, right? There's another international train station in Paris, the Gare de Lyon. I bet that's where they're headed."

Paul tilted his head. "A fiver? You're betting on MI6s reputation, Evie."

"Tenner?"

"Fine." Paul smirked. "A tenner."

The travel time to Gare de Lyon was normally twenty minutes. The way both taxis were speeding, they'd probably make it there in half that.

Watching the streets of Paris fly by, Paul said, "If you have a chance to take Bourke, do it. We'll find a way to get him out of the country. If we're awfully lucky, his previous employment status will never be uncovered." He paused. "But do not apprehend her."

Eva stared at Paul. He didn't turn to face her.

"Don't look at me like that, Evie."

"You don't even know how I'm looking at you."

"Yes I do." He finally faced her. "We're just after Alex. We leave her alone."

"What? Why?"

Paul sighed. "The only reason we were invited to that little junket back there was because I agreed we wouldn't harm or detain Isabella in any way."

"I didn't agree to that!" Eva's lips thinned. "I'm smelling something Paul, and it's something that even a fertiliser expert would say was bloody whiffy."

He sighed. "There's every chance Isabella will get off scot-free." He spoke as if he was relaying unwelcome cricket scores, with a sense of inevitability. "The DGSE won't want to deal with the mess created by one of its own. The government won't want to deal with claims that a specially trained and vetted employee blew up their own citizens, especially not during an election year. The ramifications would be too great, the collateral damage too costly. Imagine the testimony if it went to court. The DGSE and French intelligence wouldn't live this down for years. MI6 is still living down Philby and the Cambridge Five, and that's nothing compared to this. Nothing. This will stain their country for a century."

Eva was too livid to answer. She couldn't believe what she was hearing. The woman who had tortured her, who had Volmer killed, who had masterminded the deaths of over one hundred of her own countrymen would walk free. It beggared belief.

Paul went on. "No, my guess is that Isabella will be quietly shunted out of the DGSE, given a slap on the wrist and a hefty pension. There will be no justice for her or her victims."

Eva stared at him in utter shock. "Surely justice for..." Her voice trailed off.

Paul took her hand and gave a weak smile. "Sometimes this profession needs to create the story the public want to hear. It's not always the right one, but it's the story that will be told."

They spent the rest of the trip in silence, the taxi in front never too far away. Eva did her best to refocus her mission. It was ironic that after all she'd been through, all the twists and turns, she was back to her original assignment. Catch Alex, the not-so-dead ex-MI6 agent.

Ahead, the traffic was getting as thick as ratatouille, Eva lost sight of their prey. They were near Gare de Lyon, Eva's hunch may well have been right, but they'd lost sight of the other taxi. The driver swore.

They'd lost them.

As they arrived at the beautiful early 20th century station they skidded to a sudden halt. The driver sighed heavily having lost them at the last stretch, and Paul threw him a wad of cash as they piled out. They ran in and Eva was momentarily awed by the beautifully ornate roof.

The station was massive, being a major hub for France rail passengers. There were two halls with many platforms, too much to cover at once. Paul stood before the huge departures board and his shoulders slumped.

"We'll need to keep an eye out, split up," he said, squinting. "We're never going to cover all the ground we need to."

Eva took a few extra moments to study the board. There were several destinations within France. Possible, but unlikely. They would want the greatest amount of distance between them and Isabella's mother country. The two next international destinations were Italy and Switzerland. Both had extradition treaties with France, but they were also international airport hubs.

"You go to Hall One, platform three," Eva said. "The Switzerland train."

Paul chortled. He would have known she'd choose the most likely for herself. "Why are you taking Hall Two?"

A shrug. "Isabella's preference for Italian wine. It's not much more than a hunch, but it will do."

Paul nodded and ran towards the first hall. Eva ran in the opposite direction. The platform was barred by a lone ticket inspector. She was cheerfully checking each passenger's ticket and wishing them a pleasant journey. When an elderly woman in a wheelchair needed to get through, the inspector went to assist her through the gate. Eva slipped through undetected. So much for covering Paris in a net. She had defeated a lone ticket inspector within two minutes.

Finding an isolated alcove on the platform, Eva watched all newcomers intently. Nearly every part of her ached. She should have been recuperating in hospital, but she had other priorities.

She bit her nails. With mere minutes before departure, she was weighing up whether she had time to speed through the train and peruse the commuters who had already boarded.

She almost missed them.

Almost.

They had changed again. Alex was dressed as a train porter, complete with peaked cap. He carried two large bags. Isabella seemed to be channelling some sort of Hollywood starlet. They must have assumed you hide best out in the open. Her hair colour may have been red, and her dress far more ostentatious than her usual style, but Eva would know that walk anywhere.

The two spies boarded the train as the inspector blew her whistle. Departure was imminent. Eva pulled out her phone and called Paul. She told him what she knew.

"I'm on my way."

"You better run, dude."

Paul was already breathing heavily. "Won't it appear suspicious if I'm running through a train station?"

Eva laughed quietly. "Carry a fire extinguisher. Nobody's going to stop a bloke carrying a fire extinguisher."

A quick glance at the platform clock told Eva he wasn't going to make it.

"Do I get on, boss? It's leaving."

The train blew its whistle. The engine shunted. The only response from Paul was a series of grunts as he ran.

"Paul? On or off?"

The train's whistle blew twice more.

"Paul?"

Paul let out an exasperated sigh. "Do it."

Eva ran at the train and leapt on just as the automatic doors slid shut. She was on. Through the doors she could see Paul at the gate, arguing with the inspector as he pointed at the train.

The train sped up and Eva made her way through the carriage. Alex and Isabella had entered two carriages ahead. A sleeper car. Thanks to the money they'd accumulated through the deaths of others, they could easily afford first class.

Eva assessed her situation. No gun, it had been left behind in Isabella's hideout. No backup, once again. She was still weak from her recent ordeal. Alex may have a few years under his belt, but he was strong, and an experienced agent. And she knew exactly how vicious Isabella could be.

A text message from Paul simply read, "Do what you have to." Calling in the French authorities would mean they would apprehend Alex and implicate a former MI6 agent in terrorist acts. They couldn't let that happen. Eva had to capture him herself.

She was outgunned. It was time to get clever. Somehow.

Within half an hour, the sky outside grew dark. Eva walked through the dining car, past seated passengers settling in for the long journey ahead.

After two hours, most movement ceased and the kitchen shut down. Nearly everyone had bunkered down as the novelty of the train journey waned. People put themselves to bed or made themselves comfortable in their seats.

Always vigilant for any sign of Alex or Isabella, Eva was careful to appear at ease wandering around the train, as if she was simply stretching her legs. After enough time had passed, she cautiously made her way to the first-class sleeper cabins. The train carriage was modern, but not overly opulent; functional comfort. Windows down one side, the cabins down the other. Walking tentatively up the hallway, she noted that all had their doors open or windows blinds not totally down, except one.

Eva staked out a spot at the far end of the carriage and waited. It took a while, but she finally managed to catch a glimpse of Alex returning to the end cabin. As he entered, he rubbed the large bandage on his neck. He disappeared from view with a yawn. Being a bastard must have tuckered him out. *The poor dear.*

Now she knew which cabin Alex and Isabella were in. There was a small niche behind it, away from the prying eyes of fellow passengers. In that little alcove, an air vent high on the wall led into the cabin.

A full-frontal assault would be useless. Eva had fighting skills, but she was drained. No matter how good the element of surprise was, the other two would soon overpower her. Eva had no intention of being in that situation again.

How could she use their cabin to her advantage? She smirked. It would take some doing, but she had them. Eva's plan was to turn the sleeper car into a real sleeper car. Well, one cabin in particular.

Waiting until most train chatter had died down, Eva went to work.

The kitchen was locked, but that meant nothing to her. Using her lock picks, she was in within seconds. The industrial kitchen was eerily quiet. She was careful not to disturb any of the pots and pans, to avoid making any noise.

It took her a while to find what she needed. She stuffed a collection of items in her pockets, including a plastic piping bag and masking tape. The main target of her search was easy enough to find, but harder to transport.

Ensuring the passageway was clear, she hauled the heavy container down the hall. She only passed one person, a dapper old man in a suit, and in French said, "Old lady in number fifty-five is having trouble with her respiration."

He gave Eva a pleasant nod and continued on his way. The gas cylinder didn't contain oxygen. In fact, it would be used to deprive bodies of exactly that.

After enough time had passed that Eva was confident she wouldn't be disturbed, she implemented her plan. She taped the larger end of the piping bag around the cabin's air vent. She then taped the point of the bag around the end of the hose attached to the cylinder. The gas within the cylinder was LPG, or liquefied petroleum gas. Inhalation could cause dizziness, and loss of consciousness, which was what Eva was after. Two comatose spies would be easier to deal with than two angry and heavily armed ones.

The gas was denser than air, so would fall to the ground first. Eva had to be careful not to give them too much. She only wanted them to lose consciousness, not suffocate.

As Eva turned on the gas, she muttered under her breath, "Night night, you megalomaniac murderous douchepoodles."

～

The slap across Isabella's face gave Eva great pleasure. So much so, she did it again. The DGSE agent spluttered awake.

Eva watched the mental cogs turn, trying to make sense of what was happening. For Isabella, it would have been thoroughly discombobulating. One minute she'd been asleep in a cabin aboard a train, the next Eva was towering above her in something that was decidedly not that.

"Is this," she worked her jaw to bring forth saliva, "is this an ambulance?"

"Yes," Eva said brightly. "Do you like it?"

Steadily gaining consciousness, Isabella's eyes darted around the small confines of the vehicle, landing on Alex's still-unconscious form, strapped to the gurney. Her mouth opened as if she were about to say something, then closed again.

It had taken some coordinating, but Eva's employers had come through for her. Once she'd confirmed that Alex and Isabella were unconscious, she'd cleared her makeshift apparatus and raised the alarm. The train stopped at the nearest station. How MI6 had obtained an ambulance on such short notice, Eva didn't want to know.

"Where… where are we?" Isabella asked, still fighting through the fug of disorientation.

"The end of the line."

Eva opened the rear doors of the ambulance. They were inside the huge empty expanse of a warehouse. Aged concrete spread out under high rusted beams supporting a pockmarked iron roof. The old factory had been unused for decades.

"Untie Alex!"

Eva tilted her head and stared at the unconscious former-MI6 operative. "I don't think so. We have our own plans for him."

"Why am I here?" Isabella insisted in a tone far more demanding than her position would logically allow.

"Because of what you've done, Isabella," Eva said, shoving her forward. "Because of all the people you killed, the innocent lives wiped out. And for corrupting young boys to blow themselves up for your profit, and for their families, who will never see them again."

Isabella laughed. It was a hoarse, pitiless laugh. "Those people are filth. They deserve all they get."

Eva elbowed Isabella forward, and she landed on her feet at rear of the ambulance. With an extra shove, Isabella cleared the end of the emergency vehicle.

"Why don't you tell them yourself?"

Standing in a huddled group, about thirty people, mostly men, glowered at Isabella. They were all of Middle Eastern descent. They were angry. In fact, they appeared ready to riot.

"Who," Isabella spluttered, "are these people?" Fear rearranged her delicate features.

Eva grinned an unkind smile. "These fine people are the parents, brothers, sisters, cousins and uncles of the men you sacrificed in the name of free market capitalism."

Isabella's forehead creased in terror. It was ironic that someone who had spread so much herself was now overcome by it.

"They are the families of Mustafa Khoury, Nur Hakim and all the others you killed in your sick little game. These are the relatives of the boys you corrupted and murdered for your own ends. They want to have a little chat."

As if on cue, members of the posse rattled chains and slammed pieces of wood against their palms. The horror on Isabella's face was complete. She scrambled into Eva's arms and grasped the front of her top.

"They will kill me!" she screeched. "Do you 'ave no 'eart?"

Eva tilted her head at Isabella and repeated the advice she'd heard recently. "You have to be heartless to be a spy, Isabella."

She nodded and two heavy-set members of the group stepped forward and grabbed Isabella by the arms. They dragged her, kicking and screaming, towards the seething group.

Eva turned and walked away.

When Eva had started her mission, she was unsure if she and espionage were the right fit for one another. Now she'd saved MI6's reputation and completed her original assignment. Alex would be delivered with a bright red bow to headquarters. MI6 would use him to clean up any remaining threads from The Tempest organisation, if there were any. After that, she didn't care what happened to him.

With no suspect to parade around in front of the cameras, the French authorities would be forced to concede their dragnet had failed and they had let their prime suspect escape. There were no other witnesses, other than Eva's testimony that Alex was one of the two main culprits behind the bombings.

As for Isabella, if handed over to the French authorities she would never be forced to pay for her crimes. If she was brought back to MI6, it would be a diplomatic time bomb. The DGSE would demand MI6 return her, risking both organisations being linked to acts of terror.

For everyone concerned, it was best if Alex and Isabella simply disappeared. There was little doubt in Eva's mind that the authorities would find someone to blame for the atrocities. The public would demand it. It wouldn't be the real parties, though. Lies would be created, sacrifices made and the world would move on. As always, few would ever know the truth.

Eva had certainly made mistakes on her mission, taken extravagant chances with her own life and those of others, but there was one thing she was certain of.

Eva Destruction was a spy.

As she strode towards the ambulance, the first morning rays poked through the holes in the roof. Then the screaming commenced. Isabella pleaded for mercy. She cried out for compassion, for pity.

Eva tried to determine how she felt. After much deliberation, she decided she was hungry. She started the engine, wondering if that café in Lyon would be open yet.

The End

~

Want to read more about the Eva Destruction series?
Sign up to Dave's **VIP Readers Group** for more Eva news and special offers:
davesinclair.com.au/newsletter

ABOUT DAVE SINCLAIR

Dave Sinclair is a novelist, a screenwriter and a really excellent parallel parker.

He lives in Melbourne, Australia with his two crazy daughters. He's also an award-winning filmmaker, a title that sounds far more impressive than it really is. He won a best comedy screenplay and cinematography award for a short film he wrote and directed, though at the time he didn't really know what cinematography was. A completed screenplay is currently doing the rounds.

Dave's overflowing bookshelves include many works by Douglas Adams, P.G. Wodehouse, Dashiell Hammett, Raymond Chandler, Janet Evanovich, Ian Fleming, Zadie Smith and John le Carré.

The Eva Destruction books are stories Dave wanted to read, full of action, laughs and fascinating characters. Eva has many more adventures up her tattooed sleeves.

To find out more, you can stalk Dave at his semi-reputable website: https://davesinclair.com.au

www.ingramcontent.com/pod-product-compliance
Lightning Source LLC
Chambersburg PA
CBHW021432110726
47901CB00008B/2398